PROMISES OF TOMORROW

PROMISES OF TOMORROW

SHELLEY SHEPARD GRAY

THORNDIKE PRESS
A part of Gale, a Cengage Company

Copyright © 2020 by Shelley Shepard Gray
Thorndike Press, a part of Gale, a Cengage Company.

ALL RIGHTS RESERVED
This book is a work of fiction. Any references to historical events, real people, or real places are used fictitiously. Other names, characters, places, and events are products of the author's imagination, and any resemblance to actual events or places or persons, living or dead, is entirely coincidental.
Thorndike Press® Large Print Christian Fiction
The text of this Large Print edition is unabridged.
Other aspects of the book may vary from the original edition.
Set in 16 pt. Plantin.

LIBRARY OF CONGRESS CIP DATA ON FILE.
CATALOGUING IN PUBLICATION FOR THIS BOOK
IS AVAILABLE FROM THE LIBRARY OF CONGRESS

ISBN-13: 978-1-4328-8065-1 (hardcover alk. paper)

Published by arrangement with Gallery Books, a division of Simon & Schuster, Inc.

Printed in Mexico
Print Number: 01   Print Year: 2020

Our lives are like quilts — bits and pieces, joy and sorrow, stitched with love.

— Amish proverb

Thanks be to God for His gift that is too wonderful for words.

— 2 Corinthians 9:15

PROLOGUE

December 1

Even though a good amount of time had passed, Marie Hartman Byler still felt Andy Warner's absence a lot of the time. Sometimes she thought she noticed his loss more than the rest of the Eight — their large group of longtime friends.

Though they'd all been close from the time their mothers had dropped them off for day care at Mrs. Kurtz's house in the summers, only she and Andy had attended school together. The two of them had shared teachers, classrooms, and a large group of English friends all the way until they'd graduated high school.

Andy had been a constant in her life, a friend who had helped her through biology and chemistry. The boy she'd watched play football. The boy who'd stood by her side when she'd been crowned homecoming queen. Andy had known all her faults and foibles but had still liked her anyway.

Even though two years had passed, there were still times when she'd feel his loss as if he'd died just a few days before.

Like right that very moment.

She and her husband, John, plus the rest of the Eight were standing in Andy's parents' beautifully bedazzled living room. Not only did the Warners have their ten-foot tree already decorated in silver and gold, but the whole house also looked like something out of a Christmas catalog.

Then, again, Mrs. Warner had always gone all out for their annual "It's December!" holiday party. Except for last year, they'd thrown the festive party the first weekend of December for as long as Marie could remember. It was always a lot of fun, and everyone had gone — even their Amish and Mennonite friends.

Marie had felt so awkward about

going without Andy that she and John had almost made other plans. But when they realized that the rest of the Eight — and all their parents — were going, Marie had gone out and bought a new blue velvet dress.

Seeing everyone had been good. Really good. Mr. and Mrs. Warner had given Marie warm hugs. All of the Eight's parents were standing in a group catching up, just like they always had. But for the last hour, she, John, and the rest of the Eight had been struggling. Oh, they'd eaten the tasty prime rib sliders, caught up with one another, and admired the Warners' grand piano, which played Christmas music by itself. However, as the minutes passed, it was getting harder and harder to act as if it was okay that Andy wasn't standing with them.

She and John had just finished their plates of food and were sitting down in the Warners' game room when Katie, Harley, and their new baby joined them.

"I think we're going to leave soon," Harley said as he sat down on the couch beside John.

Marie was surprised. Their baby was sound asleep in Katie's arms. Katie usually tried not to wake him if she didn't have to. "You're going to wake up Kevin."

Harley shrugged. "As grumpy as he'll be, I'm hoping it will help him sleep tonight."

John frowned. "Aren't your parents still here?"

"*Jah,* but they don't need us," Harley replied. "They're sitting with the Warners and the Clarks."

Though she felt bad about leaving early, if Katie and Harley were going to leave, maybe she and John could sneak out too. "My parents have been hanging out with them too," Marie said. She covered her mouth when a yawn escaped her. "Sorry, I don't know what's wrong with me. I can hardly stay up until ten right now."

"That's because you've been working overtime, shopping for Christmas, and getting ready for our big camping trip," John chided. Turning to the other couple, he continued. "I've told Marie at least a dozen times that she needs to stop trying to do everything. She never listens."

Harley grinned at Logan and Tricia when they approached. "Hi, you two. I was just about to go find you."

"Oh? What's going on?" Logan asked.

"The four of us are going to leave soon," Katie explained. Smiling down at her baby, she said, "I mean, the five of us."

Tricia looked crestfallen. "Do you all really have to go so soon?"

"I mean no offense to your parents, Trish," Marie hastened to explain. "This is a lovely party."

"It's not that." After glancing at Logan, Tricia explained. "I actually came down here to get you all."

"Because?" John asked.

"All of our parents asked that you join them." Looking more than a little awkward, she swallowed. "Everyone is gathered around . . ."

Marie was starting to get a bad feeling. "Trish, what's going on?"

"You know what I'm asking. My parents, well, a lot of our parents, are asking for one of us to share a story about the Eight."

John frowned. "I don't think this is the best time for that."

"As a matter of fact, I think it might be," Tricia said. "The stories you all share about growing up together always help my parents. They help all of us a lot, if you want to know the truth." Her voice softened. "As the months pass, I think it's tempting for us all to try to make Andy into something he really wasn't. You all sharing your memories helps us remember the way Andy really was." She gazed at all of them. "Please, will one of you tell a story?"

Taking hold of his wife's hand, Logan looked at the rest of the Eight. "Tricia has a good point. Can't someone step up?"

"I'm sorry, but I'm not up for it tonight," Katie said. "I spoke at your brother's funeral, and it just about killed me." Wincing, she closed her eyes. "I didn't mean to just say that."

"E.A. spoke at Marie and John's wedding. And Kendra spoke at the anniversary of his death," Logan said. "What do you think, Marie? Could you share a story tonight?"

"Why me?" Marie asked. Feeling panicked, she turned to her husband. "John, couldn't you talk tonight?"

"Um, I don't think so. You would be much better."

She glared at her husband. "Oh, John. Really?"

"Sorry, but I have to say, I don't think this is John's thing," Logan said. "You know how he gets shy in front of people he doesn't know. He mumbles and fidgets. No one can figure out what he's trying to say half the time."

"It's true," John said. "I hate standing up in front of big groups

16

of people. Within five minutes, I'll be stumbling over every word."

"I agree with Logan," Harley said quietly. "Marie, you'd be the best person to speak tonight. After all, you and Andy did a lot more together than the rest of us."

It was like Harley had just read her mind about how much she'd missed Andy. Setting down the cup of punch she'd been sipping, she sighed. "I'm not going to get out of this, am I?"

"Nope," Harley said, getting to his feet. "But I have to admit that I'm kind of looking forward to what you have to say."

Marie thought of one story that always made her smile, but she just wasn't sure it was suitable. "Hey,

Trish?"

"Hmm?"

"What if I told about the time I decided to host a Christmas party and Andy brought Stephanie?"

Tricia smiled so broadly, her whole face lit up. "That would be awesome. I had almost forgotten about Stephanie. Yes, do tell that story. It's a *gut* one."

"I *canna* believe you're going to tell everyone that," Katie said, visibly trying not to laugh.

Looking at them all, Marie started having second thoughts. Like most of their tales, it didn't exactly put any of them in the best light. She lowered her voice. "Tell me the truth, guys. Is it in poor taste?"

John surged to his feet. "Oh, *jah.*"

"Okay, then." She was actually kind of relieved. Maybe Logan could talk or something . . .

"But I can't wait for you to tell everyone about it," John added. "It's going to be grand."

Still feeling hesitant, Marie added, "I better warn you all that even my parents don't know everything that happened that night."

"Mine don't either," John replied.

This wasn't making her feel better. "You know what? I sure would hate to embarrass Mrs. and Mr. Warner —"

"Oh, my parents already know some of what happened," Tricia said as she led the way upstairs, Katie and Logan at her heels.

"They do?" she whispered to

Harley. "Did you know that?"

Harley folded his hands behind his back. "Marie, Stephanie got a black eye that night, and Andy went home with a pair of guinea pigs. Of course Mr. and Mrs. Warner knew about it."

Oh, boy. So, she wasn't even going to be able to gloss over the worst parts. She was going to have to tell the whole, embarrassing story. All of it, from beginning to end.

"There you all are," Mr. Warner said as they approached. "Did Tricia ask you for our favor?"

"Yes, sir," Marie said. "We, um, came up with a story to share."

"So, who is going to do the honors this time?" Harley's father asked. As usual, his expression was stoic, but his eyes were warm.

"Me. I mean, I am," Marie said as she walked through the maze of people. There had to be almost eighty people in the room. All of their parents, most of their siblings, people Tricia and Andy had gone to school with, and a group of the Warners' neighbors.

After glancing over at John, who had sat down next to his sister Molly's wheelchair, Marie pinned a smile on her face.

"Hello, everyone. My name is Marie Byler. Happy December! Thank you, Mr. and Mrs. Warner, for putting on this lovely party again. Everything has been wonderful. As wonderful as it always has been."

She paused, worried that everyone would know how hard she was trying not to talk about how much she missed Andy.

"Go ahead, Marie," Nate called out. "Tell us a good story about Andy and the Eight at Christmastime."

Smoothing her hands down the fabric of her dress, Marie contemplated where to start.

And then it was so perfectly obvious.

"All of you know we Eight grew up going to a lot of these parties at Andy's house."

"Every year, your whole group would run around and laugh, always thick as thieves," Mrs. Warner called out.

"But far louder," Mr. Warner added with a playful wince.

"Yes, that sounds about right. But, what you might not know, is that back when we were all sixteen and seventeen, we decided we needed our own party."

"I remember that night well," Marie's mom called out.

Realizing that she was about to learn some new information, Marie cleared her throat. "I decided to host a party for the Eight at my house — well, the Eight and about a dozen of our other friends. And Stephanie," she added, because she never categorized her as a friend.

"Oh, boy," Mr. Warner said. "I had almost forgotten about that girl. My word, but she loved to give Andy the runaround. That girl was certainly a handful."

Marie nodded. Yes, indeed, Stephanie had been that.

Of course, now that she was older, Marie figured that all of them had been a handful back when they were sixteen and seventeen. "As you might have guessed, that Christmas party didn't turn out the way we expected."

"Oh, honey. They never do," Mrs. Warner said with a smile.

Marie smiled back. Andy's mother was exactly right.

1

"I guess it's the nature of things, but back then, by the time we were seventeen or so, the eight of us had drifted apart. Because they were Amish, Logan, John, and Harley had finished school years before and were working on their farms. E.A. was at her private Mennonite school, preparing to graduate at the top of her class and winning all kinds of academic awards. Andy and I were at the public high school. I was trying to figure out where to go to college. And . . . Andy?

"Well, Andy had a new girlfriend named Stephanie."

Three Weeks Later
Marie, John, E.A., Will, Kendra, and Nate had been at the large cabin in the woods outside of Walnut Creek for exactly two hours. The other four had hired a driver and were due to get there any minute.

The weekend had been months in the making. Trying to figure out dates that everyone could agree on, transportation, and meals had been quite an undertaking. By the time Marie was able to reserve a cabin big enough for ten, the nicest ones had been taken. She'd picked out the best-looking one that was still available. But in person, their home away from home for the next three days didn't look so good. Not at all.

E.A.'s expression when she'd first stepped inside the cabin had said it all. She'd looked like she regretted ever saying yes to Marie's idea of a fun, relaxing couples' getaway.

Marie supposed she couldn't blame her.

Their monster of an A-frame cabin was far more depressing-looking and dingier than the pictures she'd viewed online. The laminate countertops were cracked and stained, the three bathrooms were tiny and barely functional, and some of the furniture looked like it had come from the clearance section of a secondhand store.

Looking at it all through fresh eyes, Marie felt like crying. She wouldn't blame a single one of her friends if they never spoke to her again. Everyone had made a lot of sacrifices with their time to make this trip happen. Some of them had even left their children with relatives so they could relax and have a good time.

But this? Well, it was a far cry from the "fancy" Airbnb cottage in the woods they'd all originally planned to stay in. Instead, they were making due in a rustic cabin that seemed to be stuck in the year

1975. Hiking wasn't even going to be much of an option if the snow kept falling much longer.

Always one to problem solve, Marie sat down on one of the four wicker stools tucked under the kitchen counter. Looking around, she attempted to figure out how to make things look better. But so far, she was coming up empty.

"You never told me how your room was up in the attic," Kendra said as she entered the kitchen and sat down on the rickety stool next to Marie. "Is it all right?"

Just thinking about the room, which could only be reached by climbing a steep set of stairs, made her grimace. She wasn't feeling all that great, so that second set of stairs felt almost insurmountable. "Not really. It's hot up there, and it was fairly dusty." There had also been spiderwebs, but she wasn't going to mention that. "John already pulled the awful bedspread off of the mattress and checked for bedbugs."

Kendra looked alarmed. "Did he find any?"

And *that,* right there, was exactly why Marie feared she was going to be completely without any of her best friends on Christmas Day. Kendra wasn't exaggerating at all — the creatures were a legitimate concern.

She cleared her throat, attempting to get rid of the lump that was forming. "No. The sheets looked clean, thank goodness. Not a bed-bug in sight." She smiled wanly. "How is your room?"

Kendra smiled. "It's all right. Good enough, I think. The lantern has kerosene, and the towels on the chair by our window smelled good. It's obvious someone washed them recently. It didn't occur to me to pull off the bedspread, but I'll ask Nate to help me do that and check for bugs when he comes back inside." Brightening, she said, "I'll tell the others to do that too."

Marie covered her face with her palms. "Kendra, I'm so sorry about the condition of everything. I feel terrible that I talked everyone into this place."

"Don't be so hard on yourself,

Marie. It's not like it took all that much talking or convincing. We all wanted to be here. Plus, it's not your fault it took the ten of us so long to make concrete plans."

Somehow that reminder made their situation even worse. They'd had such great plans! "I promise, I never imagined that this place would be so . . . rustic."

"Sorry, but I think *rustic* means kind of primitive-looking." Looking around them, at the furniture that was straight out of the 1970s, the avocado green appliances that looked like they hadn't been serviced in decades . . . the broken window that was boarded up, Kendra chuckled. "This is something else."

Just as Marie was about to agree, E.A. entered the kitchen.

"This is what?" E.A. asked.

"Nothing," Marie said quickly. E.A. was one of her dearest friends, but she also was extremely organized and smart. She was the kind of woman who would call every single reference on the Airbnb site before booking.

Unfortunately, Marie was not.

Kendra looked at her sympathetically then turned to E.A. "We were just talking about the state of this place."

"Oh. Well, it's dirty, worn, and freezing," E.A. said as she peered into the fireplace. "I sure hope this works. If it doesn't, we're going to be miserable."

"The men went outside to gather wood," Kendra said.

"There's plenty of that around. Stacks and stacks of it against the walls." E.A. wrinkled her nose. "I hope they don't bring in any mice."

"I hadn't thought about that. I bet there are quite a few nestled in those stacks outside," Kendra murmured. Eyeing the brick chimney that went all the way to the top of the cabin, she said, "I guess we should hope and pray that no birds are nesting inside."

Just thinking about birds squawking and flying into the cabin made Marie feel sick. Everything was going from bad to worse, and she hadn't even thought that was possible.

"I don't know what to do," she murmured. "I wanted us to all get together but not like this. All everyone is going to do is complain." Of course, what she was really worried about was everyone getting mad at her and making an already disappointing weekend even worse. But Marie wasn't brave enough to mention that.

"We might not *all* complain," Kendra said.

"But there's a pretty good chance that most of us will," E.A. joked. Turning to Marie, her expression softened. "Oh, Marie, don't take it so hard. I'm pointing out the obvious, but I'm not blaming you. Everyone speaking their minds can't be helped, you know. It's the nature of us." Her eyes lit with amusement. "We know each other too well."

Marie couldn't argue with that. Maybe E.A. did have a point. They all felt so comfortable with one another that they could say anything they wanted to without fear of it being passed on to other people. Who else in her life valued such trust and honesty?

She never dared to be completely candid with her parents. Her mother would be crushed if Marie ever admitted half the things she thought from time to time. "Um, I guess that is true. I kind of like that we have that sort of relationship."

Kendra smiled encouragingly. "Me too."

The door opened, bringing in John and Nate. Both looked a little shell-shocked, and neither was carrying any wood.

"I thought you were going to bring in firewood," E.A. said as she walked toward them. "Oh, no! Was none of it usable?"

John and Nate exchanged glances. "It was plenty usable," John said.

"Well then, what happened?" Marie asked as she hopped down from her stool. "Uh-oh. Were there lots of mice nesting inside the logs? I hate when that happens. They scurry around and scare me half to death."

"No, it wasn't that," Nate said. He looked like he was about to say more but instead looked at John.

"Nate, what did happen?" Kendra asked. She'd hopped off her stool but was still standing near the kitchen.

Nate walked to her side and wrapped an arm around her shoulders. "We did see a few rodents, but it wasn't anything odd. The mice seemed well, like mice. Nothing out of the ordinary."

When Marie noticed Nate kiss Kendra's brow, she began to fear the worst, though she had no idea what that could possibly be. "I'm sorry, but I still don't understand. I thought you guys were going to bring in some wood."

E.A. nodded. "And why are you two in here but not Will? Where's my husband?"

"He's still outside," John replied. "You see, we found someone."

"You found a person? Like a stranger?" E.A. frowned.

"*Jah.* A woman," John said. "Will's speaking with her now." He peeked out the window. "And probably Katie, Harley, Logan, and Tricia as well, by the looks of things." Turning back to Marie, he explained. "The driver was dropping them off when Nate and I decided to come inside to tell you ladies about this new development."

It was becoming obvious that there was quite a bit more to this story. "John, you are kind of making this woman sound like she's a lost puppy."

He glanced out the window. "Um,

jah . . . though it ain't quite the same, is it?"

"No. No, it is not." E.A. cleared her throat. "If you found this woman, was she lost? Or did she just happen to be walking by?"

"Oh, she's lost, all right," Nate answered. "I'm thinking she might be lost in more ways than one, you know?"

Kendra shook her head. "I'm sorry, but I'm not following you."

"Will is hoping to convince her to come inside and join us for the night," Nate shared. "It's getting on three o'clock. It will be dark before you know it."

Marie sighed. Nate was right. December in central Ohio meant that the skies started to darken around four o'clock. It wasn't safe for anyone to be out in the woods alone.

E.A. strode toward the window and peeked out. "Logan and Harley are in my way. I can't see what she looks like." As if she realized how she sounded, she cleared her throat. "Not that it matters."

"She needs a friend right now," Nate said.

"Yes, of course," Marie murmured.

Kendra went to stand by E.A., and John and Nate strode to the kitchen. But Marie stayed put. She knew she would do whatever the poor woman needed, but she was human enough to allow herself to be disappointed for a moment or two.

It was all so very unexpected and confusing. It wasn't that she didn't want to help the poor girl, but she also didn't want to get involved with some random woman. There had to be a reason she was all by herself. Maybe she was in trouble? Maybe she had a drug problem? The news was filled with stories of men and women who had gotten embroiled in the opioid epidemic and were now mere shadows of their former selves.

John had such a good heart and had led a fairly sheltered life. He might not see the signs that she would.

If that was the case, she was going to drive the woman straight to the police station. Officers there could help her find a shelter or whatever she was looking for.

"Marie?" John said quietly. "Are you with me?"

"I am, as long as this woman doesn't look like trouble."

"I don't think so. Um, she kind of just looks lost, and maybe a little sad too."

"Is she English or Amish?" E.A. said.

"She's English." Marie's husband smiled at her softly. "As English as my Marie."

Normally, such words would make her melt. But at the moment, all Marie cared about was having one thing about their vacation go right, and that meant getting rid of their interloper. "If she's that lost, I'll drive her to wherever she needs to go. If we left now, I bet I could get back before it gets too late."

"*Nee,* Marie," John said. "I don't want you out tonight."

"John, I'll be fine."

"The snow is coming down harder. I don't think that's a *gut* idea either, Marie," Kendra murmured.

E.A. nodded. "*Jah.* This woman is simply going to have to stay here with us tonight. And, if the weather gets as bad as the forecasters hinted, it might be for more than just one night."

So, they were going to have a lost English girl with them for at least the next twenty-four hours. A girl they didn't know anything about, including where she came from or how she ended up in the woods all by herself. All Marie's planning and good intentions had been for nothing. Everything she'd hoped would happen — reconnecting with one another, relaxing before the craziness of Christmas, even taking time to remember Andy and reflect on all that had happened in the last two years — well, if this stranger was in their midst, it wouldn't stand a chance.

She didn't want to be heartless, but she knew that some people, whether they were Amish or English, were trouble.

What if that was what this woman was like? She could cause all sorts of problems for them. Worse, they'd be alone with her in a dark cabin in the middle of a snowstorm.

There would be nowhere else for them to go.

2

"It wasn't that we didn't like Stephanie; it was that Stephanie didn't understand Andy's friendship with all of us," Marie continued.

"Marie, sorry, but that isn't exactly the truth . . ." Katie called out.

"All right, fine." Looking at the audience, Marie said, "The truth is that none of us liked her much,

47

but we were trying. Because, you see, Andy liked her a lot."

This was, without a doubt, the stupidest thing she'd ever done, Elizabeth Trainor decided.

Or at least, it was in the top five. It was definitely right up there with trying to ride her Amish neighbor's goat when she was five. That goat had kicked her hard enough to land her in the hospital with a broken leg.

But what she'd just done during the last forty-eight hours? Lying to her family and friends about where she was going? Renting a cabin that was little more than a shack with spiders, getting lost in a snowstorm . . . and now actually thinking about spending the night in a cabin in the middle of nowhere with a group of strangers?

She felt a tremor climb her spine.

Yes, this was easily ten times worse. She was going to be lucky if the worst thing that happened was a broken bone. After all, she'd seen plenty of crime shows. They could only be pretending to be nice Amish people. This group could be planning to kill her and then bury her in a pit out back.

"Elizabeth?" The somber-looking man with kind eyes spoke, jarring her out of her downward spiral. "It's mighty cold out, *jah*? Let's get you inside."

Beth blinked. "Oh. Yeah. Sure."

He gestured for her to precede

him.

Each step felt like she was wading through concrete, she was so nervous. Fearing that he could tell she was kind of afraid of going inside, she turned back toward him. "I'm glad you speak English."

His lips twitched. "Me too. My name is Harley." He gestured to a girl around her age in a dark green dress. "This here is Tricia."

"Hi. My name is Elizabeth, but I go by Beth," she said as they walked inside the cabin. The room was huge, with two seating areas and a fireplace situated in between them. Just beyond the living space was a big table and a rather small-looking kitchen nook.

"I only just became Amish," Tricia said.

"So you speak English too?"

"Everyone here speaks English. Most Amish do," Tricia explained.

Feeling like everyone was listening, Beth apologized. "Sorry, I didn't know that."

Actually, she didn't know of any Amish who hung out with people who were English, or vice versa. It was hard to wrap her head around this group, which seemed so at ease with such diversity.

"Of course you wouldn't," Tricia murmured. "I mean, not unless you actually knew Amish people."

"I do know a couple of Amish people. I didn't talk to them too much, so I wasn't sure if they knew a lot of English words." She inwardly winced. She probably just managed to offend everyone in the room.

Leaning close, Tricia lowered her voice. "Try to relax, Beth. I promise, everyone isn't as different as you might think."

Not knowing what to say about that, Beth smiled tightly as she pulled a lock of hair back behind her ear.

Harley frowned at her. "Your hand is all bloody."

It was? Holding it out in front of her, Beth gazed at it like it belonged to someone else. She had a pretty good cut, that was for sure. Without stitches, it was going to scar. Realizing that Harley was still frowning at her, she dropped her hand

and scanned the worn wood. "Oh, no. Am I dripping on your floor?"

"If you were, it wouldn't hurt anything," one of the men said, reminding Beth that she was now standing in the midst of a bunch of strangers. Even though she was trying hard to be brave, she tensed up again.

Tricia chuckled softly. "Don't mind my husband. Logan is always joking around. Come on. Let's get it washed off," she said as she led Beth through the group of people. "What happened?"

"I slipped on some ice and cut my hand on the edge of a rock. It's nothing." At least the cold air had helped her injury.

Another woman joined them and

turned on the sink. Without saying a word, she directed Beth's hand under the stream of water. "Boy, you've had a bad day, huh?"

"Yes." And calling it a bad day wasn't even the half of it. She'd had a bad three months. They'd been terrible. The worst of her life.

"I'm Kendra," a friendly-looking girl with wide brown eyes said. "Nice to meet you."

"Nice to meet you too. I'm sorry I ruined your party."

She shrugged like it didn't matter. "No worries. We get together a lot. I'm just glad you found us. You could have gotten hurt, or worse, out there by yourself."

"The snow really was coming down. Hopefully I'll be able to

leave first thing tomorrow morning."

Kendra shrugged again, as if it didn't matter to her one way or the other.

The woman was being so nice. Everyone was. Beth knew she needed to be less guarded, less quiet, but she just didn't know if she had that in her at the moment. All she felt like she could do was not freak out. In her experience, people often said things they didn't mean or led her to believe they were supportive or kind when all they did was act against her when her back was turned.

Beth didn't know if these people were like that or not, but in her mind, it didn't even matter. She was stuck in a cabin full of strangers. They were probably going to ask her all kinds of questions, then make sure she knew how dumb she'd been to take a walk by herself in the woods during a snowstorm. She was going to have to sit there and take it too. She had no choice, since it was both snowing and frigid outside.

No doubt, they weren't going to waste any time judging her. She probably deserved it too. She was nineteen years old and had made one terrible decision after another over the last two days.

After lying to her parents and telling them she was still in her college dorm room, she'd used the last of her money to rent the worst place on the face of the earth for a week-end. Then, she put the directions in her phone and drove. Then drove some more in the snow.

When she'd finally arrived, after almost sliding into a clump of trees while making a right-hand turn, she'd discovered just how bad her rental cabin was.

Her "cozy, rustic cabin" was really more like an old, run-down shack. It had been filled with old blankets, rugs, and furniture that decades of hunters and who knew who else had used and probably never washed.

But the dirt and the, well, *ick factor* wasn't the worst.

No, the worst was the spiders. There had been lots and lots of spiders. So many, she'd been afraid they were going to jump on her if she sat still long enough.

She'd cried all night in the cold, wrapped up in Joel's hoodie and sweats. But this morning, things hadn't looked any better, so she'd decided to go on a walk. By herself in the woods. Without food, water, or a cell phone. After she'd fallen and hurt her hand, things had only gotten worse.

A lot worse, since she was now in a cabin filled with strangers who said they were Amish. Yet, there didn't seem to be a single horse and buggy in sight. Even she knew that didn't add up.

This had gone from stupid to bad. Really, *really* bad.

She should have planned much better. Or at least, thought things through instead of only dwelling on her pain. If Joel were still alive, he'd have been yelling at her right now, and she would be welcoming it.

And, just like he'd summoned the tears, she started crying. Again.

"Hey, it's okay," Kendra said. Calling over her shoulder, she said, "Anybody have some Band-Aids?"

"I think I've got some, Kendra," a man said. "Let me go see."

Kendra ushered her to the table and plopped her onto a chair. "We need some tissues too, Nate."

A man with light hair and hazel eyes walked to Kendra's side. "She bleeding again?"

"Crying."

"I'm okay," Beth said as the guy sat down and slid a wad of toilet paper across the table. She pulled off a couple of squares and blew her nose.

"Sorry," he said. "We didn't think of Kleenex."

Wiping at her face, she kind of half laughed. "This works. Thanks."

"I know you're scared, but Kendra and me can sleep in here. You can have our room," Nate said. "That way you can have some privacy."

"It's not that. It's um, it's been a pretty bad couple of days."

"How long were you lost?" Nate asked.

"Just a couple of hours. But I wasn't talking about that. I, well,

I've made a series of bad decisions lately. Now I'm paying the price. So are you too, I guess."

"Don't you worry about us any-more," Kendra said. "We're fine."

After another ten minutes, which had felt like an eternity, Kendra and Nate encouraged her to join the rest of the group gathered around the fire.

She still felt awkward, but their kindness and the warmth of the fire helped her relax. Maybe she was going to be all right, after all. She could sit with these people for a while, then after an hour or so excuse herself and go collapse in the bedroom they were giving her. If there weren't creepy spiders everywhere, she was going to be able to fall asleep immediately.

She couldn't wait.

Then Marie, the English woman with the beautiful golden hair, spoke. "So, Elizabeth, perhaps you could tell us how you happened to end up here today."

She didn't want to talk about Joel. Didn't want to share any of her pain. She knew that once she did, she wasn't going to be able to stop talking or sharing. She had so many emotions tied up deep inside her, and she wasn't sure how she was ever going to get them all out without turning into a blubbering idiot.

Yet, wasn't that how she was already acting?

"It might take a while," she warned. "I'm afraid it's kind of a long tale."

"I don't mind that," Marie said. "Tell us everything. Or, at least everything you'd like to share."

Harley, with his kind eyes, looked at her directly. "I know you don't know any of us, but I promise we're not asking to be nosy. We might be able to help in some way."

She doubted that. But, well, today had taught her that relying only on herself wasn't working out so well.

No, all keeping secrets had done was make things even worse and, obviously, make her even more alone.

It was time to share her story.

3

"My mother had let me order a tray of sandwiches and a couple of bags of chips for the party. She'd even made a raspberry sherbet and ginger ale punch so we could all have something kind of fun and fancy to drink.

"I made a cake, which almost turned out all right. To cover up the sinkhole in the center of it, I made a ton of icing. I even decided to make it look Christmasy by adding green food coloring to the icing." She looked at the crowd. "It turns out that you really don't need all that much to make it a pleasing shade. Mine, I'm sorry to say, was not that."

Their uninvited guest was sitting so uncomfortably, it looked like she was on the witness stand. Marie's heart went out to her. It was becoming apparent that they didn't have anything to fear from her. She was simply a young college girl in the middle of some kind of personal problem.

But even though it might have been kinder to leave Beth alone, that wasn't their way. They liked to help one another out. Or, in this case, get in one another's business.

Leaning against her husband, Marie gave the girl an encouraging smile. "What's been going on, Beth?"

Beth released a ragged sigh. "Like I said earlier, my name is Elizabeth Trainor. I grew up down in New Albany, and I've been going to Oberlin College for the last two years. I'm in the conservatory there."

"Do you play an instrument?" Katie asked.

"Vocal studies. I sing." The girl shook her head as if to clear it. Her long black hair fanned around her shoulders before she smoothed it away impatiently. "The reason I'm telling you this is that Oberlin is a pretty small college in the middle of farm country, really."

"I'm familiar with Oberlin," Tricia said. "I think a few of us are."

Beth took a deep breath before continuing. "I like to sing, and I like to study music. A lot. It's all I've ever wanted to do, even back in high school. And I'm pretty shy." Beth swallowed. "Maybe that's why I fell for Joel so hard."

"Joel?" John asked.

"He's my boyfriend. I mean . . . he was."

Was. So Beth was in the middle of a breakup. Things were beginning to make sense. "So, Joel fell hard for you too?" Marie asked with what she hoped was an encouraging smile.

Beth nodded. "Joel was a lot like me. He liked music, didn't like crowds, and was a little awkward too. Best of all, he didn't expect anything from me other than for me to be myself. We were kind of like two peas in a pod."

Kendra, who was sitting on the floor, curved her arms around her knees. "Nothing sounds bad about that."

Beth's eyes widened. "Oh, there wasn't! I mean, Joel was great. We were great." She bit her bottom lip, then added, "We fell in love almost immediately."

"You had love at first sight," Kendra said.

"Just about." She smiled softly. "But you know how when you're in a relationship and it feels a little tentative, like you need to take baby steps until you figure it out? It wasn't like that with us. From practically the first time we met, we got each other. It was easy."

"That's a blessing," Marie said. Noticing that some of the boys' expressions were turning bored, she tried hard not to smile. Even her wonderful John wouldn't want to hear too much more about Beth's romance with Joel.

The girl continued. "Even my parents thought our relationship was special." Her voice lifted. "It was so funny . . . ever since I told my mom that I started dating a guy and that I really liked him, she would give me all kinds of warnings. Say how I didn't know what I was doing and that no one knew what love was when they were eighteen."

Marie glanced at John. "I seem to remember being told something like that before."

He wrapped an arm around her shoulders. "We both were told that."

"When my parents met Joel, they were prepared to dislike him. They had come to college armed with a whole bunch of arguments about how I shouldn't jeopardize my future because of a guy. But within two hours, my mother whispered to me that she had been wrong. She could tell that Joel and I were a really good match."

Will cleared his throat. "So, not to be rude or anything, but what happened?"

Her eyes widened. "Oh, yeah. Sorry. I'm sure you're wondering why I'm telling you all about Joel and me falling in love." She opened her mouth, then shut it quickly. It was obvious that the words were becoming harder and harder to share.

"What happened, Beth?" Kendra prompted.

"A little over two months ago, Joel got the flu. It hit him really hard. So much that I ended up taking him to the student health center, even though everyone knows they don't do much there besides the basics."

"Did they help him?" Will asked.

Beth's expression went carefully blank. "Ah, no. They gave him some medicine that was supposed to help with the symptoms and told him to go back to his dorm room and sleep. So he did. But instead of feeling better in a couple of days, he just got worse. He was really having trouble breathing, and his fever spiked. Then he started acting strange, like he wasn't sure where he was. It . . . it was really bad."

"Oh, my word!" Marie said.

Beth nodded. "We all got really scared. I called his parents and told them what was going on. His mom drove right out."

All of them were completely focused on Beth's story now. "What happened then?" Harley asked.

"His mother put him in her car and drove him home. They live in a little town near Erie, Pennsylvania. And, um, as soon as the doctors saw Joel, they admitted him into the hospital." Beth visibly shivered before regaining her composure. "Two days later, he died."

Marie gaped at her. "Your boyfriend died from the flu?"

Beth nodded. "Everyone acts like it was just some freak accident. And it really was. Joel was healthy. I mean, it wasn't like he had some heart condition or something. He was fine, then he was sick, then he was really sick. And then, two days after his mother came down to

Oberlin and took him to the doctor, she called me to say that he'd died."

She folded her arms over her chest. "And that was it. He was mine, and then he was gone."

"I'm very sorry," John murmured. "You must have been heartbroken."

"I was. I am."

"And you're also alone now," Katie said, her expression filled with understanding.

"Yes." Beth nodded slowly. "Everyone was shocked. No one could believe it. I told my parents, and they both cried. Four days later, we all went to Erie for Joel's funeral. All I had left of him was just this black coffin." Obviously struggling to retain her composure, she added, "His parents were nice and all, but they'd never seen the two of us together. They didn't really understand how close we were."

She swiped a tear from her face. "It wasn't like they cared, anyway. I mean, I might have loved Joel, but he was their son. As far as they were concerned, I was just some girl he dated."

"What did you do then?"

"I took a week off. And then I went back to college. Oberlin is expensive, and even though I'm there on scholarship, I still have a lot to keep up with. I just kept thinking that all I had to do was get through these two months."

"It's only been two months?" Tricia asked.

"Almost three. Joel died at the beginning of October. Now it's almost Christmas. It's been the longest ten weeks of my life."

"I'm so sorry," Marie said. "I am so sorry for your loss."

"Thank you." She gave them a small smile. "I promise, I'm finally getting to why I ended up here."

"You take your time," Will said.

"No, I'm almost done. Anyway, after all that, I felt like I never got to have time to just grieve, you know?"

When several of the girls nodded, Beth continued. "As soon as I finished finals two days ago, I got on my computer, located a cabin not far from here that I could stay in for two days, and got out of there."

"But?"

"But when I got inside, I realized that I'd been had. The whole place is awful. Even worse than here." Her eyes widened. "No offense."

"None taken. We've realized that we made some mistakes about this place too," Marie replied. "The pictures online looked a lot better."

"Well, my cabin is really more of a glorified shack. It looks like a place for old men to hang out in when they go hunting or something." She shivered. "And it's infested with spiders. I'm talking lots of them. Everywhere. I could hardly close my eyes last night, I was so scared of them crawling on me."

"So you decided to walk away from it?" Nate asked.

"Oh, no. This morning, I realized that all I'd brought with me was some money for food and a couple of protein bars. I decided to look around to see if there was some kind of little country store or something nearby."

"Let me guess," Nate said. "There wasn't a single store in sight."

Beth almost smiled. "If there is, I didn't find it. I couldn't find anything that looked like a store at all. I was thinking that at least I had some silence and time to think about Joel, but then I fell and I got lost and started wandering around. And then I ended up here."

"You poor thing. You've been fighting spiders and a cold shack and you haven't eaten anything."

"I'm okay. I'm just sorry that I got so lost and bothered all of you." Her brow wrinkled. "I don't know when I'm ever going to get better. I don't know how much time has to pass in order to feel like my insides aren't broken," she said, each word running into the next. "I just wish someone could tell me why someone like Joel had to die. He was so young." She swallowed. "He was everything to me. And now I'm alone."

They all remained silent as she visibly composed herself. "I really am sorry. I promise, I'm not usually the type of person who cries all the time and tells her whole life story to strangers."

"You can cry all you want," E.A. said. "I think you're right. Maybe you needed a good cry today."

Looking around at the rest of her friends, each one staring at Beth with compassion in their eyes, Marie felt a burst of warmth inside her. "Actually, I think the Lord brought you to us for a reason," she said.

Beth swiped her eyes with a wad of toilet paper that someone had brought her. "I can't think of what that could be, unless it was to make you all think again about checking out cabins' reviews and references before you rent them on the Internet."

"No, there's another reason," Marie said. "You see, all of us have lost someone dear to us, as well."

"Really?"

"Oh, yes. His name was Andy. We were his good friends for years and years. Decades, really. We all loved him . . . and then he too died too soon."

Beth gaped at her.

"So, if you were looking for someone who might understand how you're feeling, I think the Lord just directed you to the right place," Harley said. "Beth, all of us have been feeling the very same thing you have. I can promise that you aren't alone."

4

"We also decided to have a gift
exchange. The rules were simple:
the gift had to be wrapped, it was
supposed to be something any of
us would like, and it couldn't cost
more than five or ten dollars. I
brought eight monster-size
chocolate bars. Someone else
brought two jars of homemade
salsa."

Turning to Will, Marie frowned.

"Unfortunately, one of us decided to bring a pair of guinea pigs."

"I don't understand." Beth wasn't sure what else she could say. She'd gone from reluctantly sharing her story about Joel, to being surprised by the looks of compassion and understanding she was receiving, to hearing this stunning announcement.

The youngest woman there, who had been leaning against a handsome Amish man while Beth had been talking, got to her feet. "Any of us could tell you about Andy, but I'll do the honors. Andy was my brother, you see." Her voice turned rough. "About two years ago, he committed suicide."

"Wow." Realizing how unfeeling that sounded, she struggled to find better words. "I mean, I'm sorry for your loss."

"No, I've said 'wow' a time or two, as well. Sometimes there are no appropriate words to say." She looked over to her husband. When he nodded, she continued. "I know suicide isn't the same as dying from the flu. However, I can tell you that all of us were really close to him and we loved him. We feel like we've lost not just a close friend, and in my case a brother, but also a part of ourselves."

"Tricia's exactly right," Marie added. "One day, we were at Andy's house, thinking nothing would ever change. But then it all did. He left us far too early."

Beth stared at the group of people surrounding her. They'd been able to put everything she'd been feeling but hadn't known how to describe into words. "Everyone says I need to get over him," she said hesitantly.

"Already?" Marie asked.

Beth nodded. "It wasn't like we were engaged or married or anything." Opening herself up even further, she said, "But I hate when they say that. I don't know how missing someone can be measured. Does it matter that we didn't have a label telling the rest of the world that we were in love?"

"*Nee,*" Katie said. "Grief is a private thing, *jah*?"

Kendra spoke again. "It's been a hard couple of years. We've all been struggling. We've grieved together. We've cried, told stories about the things Andy used to do that we miss. We've struggled with our guilt and regretted the things we never told him." She inhaled. "I, for one, would give a lot if I could see him for even one more day."

"We've also learned some things," Marie said. "I've learned not to take good days — or good friends — for granted. I've also learned to come to terms with the fact that some people are destined to be in our lives for only a limited amount of time. That's the Lord's will, I think."

Beth nodded. "I know what you

mean. Sometimes, I've found myself trying to make deals with God. When Joel was sick, I asked Him for one more day. Now I'd settle for one more dream that Joel is in."

"I don't know about you, but I found that it didn't really help," Marie said quietly. "The pictures and the memories and the hurt all pierced sections of our hearts. And because of that, none of us are the same."

"Did anything help?" Beth asked.

"Oh yes," Marie's husband, John, said. "Time."

"You're in the worst of it now, I'm afraid, Beth," Will murmured. "You've lost someone dear to you and there's nothing you can do to make it better besides grieve and cry."

"And then wake up and try to do something the next day," Katie added.

"Are things better for all of you now?"

The question seemed to take them all off guard, and they exchanged looks.

John spoke first. "For what it's worth, I've learned a couple of things that do help. The first is that keeping everything inside doesn't solve anything."

"Pretending not to be sad doesn't help much either," Tricia added. "All it does is push everything away to one side. Then, before long, it creeps back."

Katie nodded. "As soon as I

started admitting that I was still upset and even angry sometimes, things started to change for me."

"You think it's okay to be mad? Won't God think I'm being selfish?"

"I think we're all selfish by nature. Jesus knows that," Kendra said. "And maybe even mourning the loss of a friend is selfish, you know? Because the person we are missing is in Heaven now. What we're sad about is our loss."

"I miss him so much. And, just as bad, I miss everything we had planned. I feel like Joel's death means that all the things I've been hoping and praying to happen aren't ever going to come true."

"Maybe they aren't going to,"

Harley said. "Actually, they probably won't."

"That doesn't make me feel much better."

"Right now, it probably doesn't. However, in time, I think it will," Marie said. She smiled. "I mean, look at all of us! Not a one of us thought we'd be okay after Andy died. And though we all still miss him, his dying made other things happen for us. Maybe they would have happened anyway, but we'll never know. And you know what? We've all learned to come to terms with that in one way or another. That is something to hold on to, I think."

5

"My *mamm* really wanted those guinea pigs gone," Will said. "Bringing them to the party was a good idea."

"Oh, *nee*. Don't you blame bringing them on me, Will," his mother called out. "I would have told you that nothing good ever comes from putting tiny pigs in a gift bag with a couple of carrots and tissue paper."

After their deep conversation,

they'd gotten busy in the rustic kitchen. When they determined that the water worked fine and that the oven and small refrigerator were hooked up to a propane tank, everyone prepared the snacks they'd brought.

"Tomorrow night we're cooking a real meal," E.A. explained to Beth as she opened a cooler and pulled out a seven-layer taco dip. "Tonight, it's all about snacks."

Beth offered to help, but there wasn't much she could do, so she stood off to the side with Marie. There was a lot to see anyway. Some of the men were working on the fire. Others were organizing cans of soda and bottles of water on the countertop. An hour later, they were all lined up, holding paper plates and bowls.

Beth piled mini pizzas, taco dip, chips, and a handful of celery and carrots onto a plate. "This all looks so good, and I didn't even know I was hungry," she said to Tricia, who was in line right behind her.

Tricia grinned. "I was just thinking the same thing." After grabbing a paper towel, she added, "Come sit down with Logan and me, Beth. I almost went to Oberlin. You can tell me all about it."

She would have thought it would be a little awkward, chatting with an Amish girl about college, but she was learning that with this group, at least, there was no "right" way to be. Everyone had grown and changed and didn't judge one another. It felt shocking to be so accepted so easily.

Later, after they'd cleaned up and were all lounging on couches in front of the fire, Beth said, "It's amazing that I found you all. It's such a coincidence."

Harley sat up. "I don't know if I'd call it a coincidence as much as God intervening, *jah*?"

Harley had a good point. For the last month, Beth had been sabotaging herself, not going to class, getting further behind, getting worse grades. Only when one of her teachers talked to her did Beth realize that it didn't have to be that way.

"I guess you're right," she said

softly. "It seems He decided it was time I get back on the right track."

Tricia smiled at her husband, Logan. "That exact thing happened to each of us a time or two. Sometimes good things happen when everything is taken out of our control."

Beth liked the sound of that. Just as she was about to ask Tricia what had happened to her, she yawned. Covering her mouth with a hand, she said, "I'm sorry. I guess I'm getting tired."

John looked at his watch. "It has gotten late. It's almost eleven."

Kendra got to her feet. "Come on, Beth. I bet you're exhausted. I'll help you get settled in our room."

Maybe on another day Beth would have tried to argue or say that she would take the couch. But right at that moment, all she wanted to do was collapse. She followed Kendra gratefully.

Stepping inside their small bedroom, she smiled in surprise. It was unexpectedly charming. A quilt and down comforter covered a queen-size bed, and the room was immaculate, save for the one suitcase next to the door.

"Thank you so much. I'm really sorry about everything. Not only did I show up uninvited in the middle of your weekend, but I also brought everyone down. All I did was talk about Joel."

"You *did* show up out of the blue,

but you couldn't help that," Kendra said. "And I don't think you brought us down at all. I, personally, am kind of glad we had to take a moment to not only talk about Andy but also realize that we've come to terms with his death."

"I'll try to get out of here as soon as I can. I promise."

"When the weather clears, we'll help you get back to your cabin safe. Now, please don't worry anymore. Everything is going to be all right."

As soon as Kendra walked out and closed the door behind her, Beth sat down on the side of the bed. Yes, everything was worn, but the sheets and blankets smelled fresh, and there wasn't a spider in sight.

After removing her sweater, boots, and socks, she pulled back the covers, lay down on the bed in her T-shirt and jeans, and rested her head on the pillow. Already her eyes were heavy.

As she drifted off, she wondered when was the last time she'd given credit to God instead of mere luck or coincidence. It had surely been a while. Joel hadn't been a Christian, and though her family did go to church on Christmas and Easter, they weren't exactly faithful churchgoers.

She realized then that she hadn't ever felt she needed to be. Her life had been easy. She'd grown up surrounded by love, had done well enough in school and with her music to get accepted into the conservatory program, and had always had a few really good close friends.

And then she'd met Joel, and she'd felt as if a star had been shining on her life. Pulling up the sheets around her shoulders, she smiled. A star, indeed.

Wouldn't it be something if she opened up her heart to the Lord right when she was at her lowest point? But maybe that was what God did. He encouraged us to let Jesus in when we were ready to let Him in. She didn't think it was an accident that so many people either in hospice or in an accident found religion.

"Is that bad?" she asked the empty room. "Is it bad to finally believe in something greater than myself only when I wasn't sure if I believed in anything?"

Instead of the question begging more questions, Beth felt overcome with a sense of peace, and she drifted to sleep comforted by that. That and the knowledge that He was with her now and always had been, even when she'd been sure she was alone. This day's events had proven that to her.

"What do you think, Kendra?" Will asked as she joined the group again. "Do you think that girl is eventually going to be all right?"

Kendra thought about it for a few

seconds before replying. "I think so. She's been going through a tough time, but she seems like she's finally found her bearings. She looked almost relaxed when we were alone in there."

"I got the feeling that she's feeling better too," Marie said.

"At least she doesn't look scared to death of us anymore," Harley said. "It took a lot of convincing to help her see that we weren't scary people."

"That's probably a good thing. She needs to be a little afraid of strangers," Marie said. "To be honest, I was worried about her." Looking hesitant, she added, "I'm ashamed to admit how much I didn't want her to join us. That wasn't very nice of me, especially so close to Christmas too."

Thinking of how even the innkeeper in Bethlehem hadn't had room for Mary and Joseph, Kendra said, "I think you are in good company. It's human nature to put ourselves first. It's a dangerous world. We'd be foolish not to feel wary of strangers."

E.A. nodded. "Especially strangers who appear out of nowhere on our doorsteps." She shifted. "You know what? I'm glad Beth arrived. I think I needed to be reminded of my blessings."

"I was just thinking that she reminded me of how far we've come," John B. said.

"What do you mean?" Logan

asked.

"Well, think about how we all felt those first few months after Andy died. I, for one, was lost."

"I felt lost too," Marie murmured. "I quit my job, moved back here, and bought a duplex that my parents weren't happy about." She shook her head. "I couldn't understand why God was leading me on that path; I just knew it was the path I had to go on." Looking at John, she said, "Now, looking back on that time, I realize that I was being guided by a higher power."

Their conversation continued, each of them sharing how they'd overcome their obstacles, often by things they couldn't control. Kendra was content to listen to everyone, thinking of the many obstacles in her life that she'd had to conquer.

"Hey, Kendra?" Katie called out.

"Hmm?"

Katie shifted so her arms were wrapped around her legs. "Are you sure you and Nate don't mind sleeping in here tonight? It's not very comfortable."

Leave it to Katie to bring it up! Just to tease her, Kendra said, "Why? Are you offering your bed?"

"Nee." She slapped a hand over her mouth. "Sorry, I mean, it's been so long since I've had a full night's sleep, I've been kind of looking forward to it."

"I'm teasing. Between your baby and the inn, it's a wonder you ever sleep at all."

As the clock marched toward midnight, Kendra and E.A. pulled out the cookies and brownies they'd made and passed them around. After whispering a little while more, eventually all of them drifted to their rooms, leaving Nate and Kendra alone in front of the big fireplace.

After reaching in her bag and bringing out the pair of blankets she'd brought "just in case," Nate spread out on the floor. "Come here, Ken, and talk to me."

She moved to his side, stretching her arms as she did so. "I'm so tired, even this floor feels pretty good."

Nate smiled. "I was thinking the

same thing. I reckon we're easy to please, hmm?"

"Maybe." She smiled back at him.

"Now, tell me what's been on your mind."

"Hmm?"

"You've been quiet. And though we've certainly had a lot going on around here, you seemed more quiet than usual. Are you all right?"

"I . . . well, I have been thinking about Beth and her being so lost."

"Does her story remind you of when you were in Columbus, living all alone?"

She knew he was referring to the two years after she'd left home. She'd tried to go to school and pick up a variety of jobs, but her life had been so hard and she'd been so haunted by memories of her abusive childhood that she'd eventually turned to alcohol and drugs to try to ease the pain. "I was actually thinking about my sister Mary. She said she was coming to Christmas, but I'm not sure if she is."

"You don't think she'll do what she says?"

"She doesn't always. I know coming back to Walnut Creek is hard on her."

"She seemed okay the last time we saw her, Kendra. I'm sure she'll be there."

"I hope so. I hope she's been feeling some kind of higher power as well, guiding her to us. I think she needs it, or she won't be coming here at all."

"If the Lord can lead Beth to all of us, I think He can bring Mary back to you. You've just got to have faith, Ken."

She closed her eyes. "Well, I do have that."

6

"When everyone came over, I had them put their gifts in a large metal bin, then we all went into the kitchen for punch, sandwiches, and cake. My parents decided to give us some privacy, so they went to a neighbor's house for supper.

"Everything would've been just fine if Andy hadn't been so smitten with Stephanie. Or if Stephanie hadn't been on a diet."

Cozy in her plaid pajamas, Marie got into bed just past midnight. She was tired but also felt extremely satisfied. The cabin was a wreck, they had an extra guest, and it was snowing and snowing outside. However, against all odds, all ten of them had been able to make it. She'd been hopeful but hadn't counted on everyone being able to adjust their busy lives.

Hearing a muted conversation outside her door, she fluffed her pillow while she waited for John to come in. It was quite the adventure, all eleven of them sharing two bathrooms, especially since one was barely bigger than a closet.

They were all making do, though, and everyone was making quite a game out of it. E.A. had even suggested they draw straws to see who got to shower first. Marie had laughed so hard when Logan told her to stop trying to organize them and go stand in line!

Somehow, she'd been one of the first to take a turn in the bathroom, which had been nice. The day had been so hectic, she hadn't even had time to pull out the fresh sheets and towels she'd brought with her. Since John had been near the end of the bathroom line, Marie had gone ahead and changed the sheets and arranged their suitcases into some semblance of order.

Now, though, she was stretched out on top of all the coverings and thinking about something far different than Beth, the Eight, or how tired she was. She had quite a secret, and it was getting harder and harder to keep from John. But what a Christmas gift it was going to be for him!

When John walked in ten minutes later, he looked around the room in surprise. "You've transformed the room! How did you do that?"

She laughed. "Remember when you were complaining about me needing so much stuff for two nights away from home? All this bedding was in one of the tote bags."

After picking up his pillow that she'd brought from home and taking a whiff of the cool, clean cotton, he grinned. "Remind me to stop complaining about all your stuff."

"I'll happily do that," she teased. It had been a pretty big adjustment for John to get used to all of her "stuff." She'd been trying to live more simply, but that was easier said than done.

After neatly placing his dirty clothes in a duffel bag, he sat on the side of the bed. He leaned close and ran a hand through her hair, pausing to play with the ends that curled. "Marie, it's been quite the day. Are you all right, sweetheart?"

Whenever he said things like that, she had to remind herself not to grin like a fool. Her husband wasn't the most demonstrative of men — and especially not in front of other people. But then, there were times like this when he let his guard down because she needed him to.

And when he did that? Well, it was truly the sweetest thing.

"I am. At least, I think I am." Thinking how cute he looked wearing his green plaid pajama bottoms and gray T-shirt, she smiled up at him. "After reminding myself that everything didn't have to be perfect, I finally settled in."

Something flickered in his hazel eyes, almost as if he had a secret of his own. "*Gut.* You need to take care of yourself. You've been going a bit Christmas crazy, and that's after you work forty hours a week and plan weekend getaways for ten people."

"I'm doing fine. Well, most of the

time."

"See?"

"It's not just me I'm taking care of, you know."

His lips curved up. "Is that right? Who else are ya taking care of?"

"You, of course."

He groaned. "Marie, I think you're talking about something else too . . . ain't so?"

When he got emotional, she sometimes teased that his Amish came out. He would say phrases like "ain't so" and start speaking in Pennsylvania Dutch. She never minded; he'd already made so many changes for her.

But right at that moment, she was curious about what he was getting emotional for. "John?"

His expression warmed. "Are you going to make *me* tell you our big news?"

He was teasing her, and it was now obvious what he was referring to. He'd already learned her big secret! But, just to be sure, she hedged. "You know we promised we wouldn't give any hints about our Christmas presents."

"I haven't forgotten, but there's some things that shouldn't be kept from one's spouse, don't you think?"

"Well . . . I haven't been keeping this from you to be mean, John. It's supposed to be a surprise. A Christmas surprise."

John shifted to lean against the headboard and then pulled her closer. "Christmas is far away, *frau.*"

"Five days."

"That's too long."

"Maybe I'll tell you on Christmas Eve?" She paused, pretending to consider it.

"*Nee.* I've already been waiting too long for you to tell me."

A lump formed in her throat, both from how sweet he was . . . and from shock. "You've known about this for a while?"

"Well, I *think* I've known." He groaned. "Marie, please, put me out of my misery. Tell me about this surprise that you've been keeping so secret."

"I'm pregnant," she admitted.

The moment she said the words,

he grinned, pulled her close, and kissed her. When he pulled away at last, he was beaming. "I knew it."

"I was going to wait until Christmas Day to tell you," she said weakly. "I have a little baby onesie and everything. It was going to be the perfect gift to give you on Christmas morning."

"It's still gonna be a perfect gift, *jah*?" he asked as he pulled her into his arms again. "*Danke,* Marie."

"You're happy?"

"Oh, *jah.* I am happy. I've been mighty happy since the moment I first suspected." He pulled back a bit to see her face. "Now, tell me the truth. How are you feeling?"

"Pretty good right now."

"Right now? What about other

times?"

"Sometimes parts of me have felt kind of sore, and I've been a little nauseous from time to time."

He frowned. "I wish I would have known that."

"It wasn't worth mentioning."

He rubbed her back. "But still . . ."

On another day, at another time, she'd have asked him all about his detective work and she'd tell him about the tests and her plans and how excited she was.

But now, right at that moment, nothing mattered except their happiness and their future. They were soon going to be their own little family. A perfect family of three.

"I love you, John Byler."

"I know, Marie," he said just before he kissed her. "I promise, I always know that you love me."

"How come?"

"Because I always love you back. That's why."

7

"Stephanie hadn't been impressed with my green cake or sherbet punch, and Andy pulled out some baby carrots and celery sticks for her to eat. I felt bad for her, but what can one do? It had never occurred to me that she would need a special meal."

Beth had thought she'd feel awkward when she walked out to greet everyone the next morning, but she hadn't.

Kendra had waved her over. "Do

you drink coffee?"

"I do."

"Great, come help me work this crazy coffeemaker," Kendra said as she speared a strip of bacon and placed it neatly on a paper towel.

Kendra was working at the stove, but it seemed every inch of counter space was filled with plates and food . . . and a turkey?

After pushing a couple of buttons on the machine and figuring out the gist of it, Beth carried the carafe to the sink and rinsed it out. "I can't believe you're making such a big breakfast," she said, deciding not to mention the turkey just yet.

"There are a lot of us, and we all like to eat," Kendra said. "I hope you're hungry."

"I am, thanks." Grabbing the bag of ground coffee, she prepared the machine and turned it on. When the telltale smell of fresh coffee hit the air, she felt a deep burst of satisfaction. Was there anything better than that first cup of coffee?

"Oh, *gut*! You figured it out," Katie said as she entered the room.

"I'm a college student. Knowing how to make coffee in any situation is almost a prerequisite," Beth joked.

"I bet." Katie walked over to the oven. "Ah, it's heated up at last." She opened a large cooler and pulled out a casserole dish. "Open the oven for me, will ya, Beth?"

She did as Katie asked. "What's that?"

"Oven French toast. I make it all the time at my bed-and-breakfast."

"It's amazing," Kendra said as she turned off the burner on the stove. "I hope this is enough."

There had to be at least two pounds of bacon on the plate. "You all sure know how to eat."

Katie giggled. "Today is our big eating day. We'll start out with a big breakfast, then end it with a turkey dinner."

Beth eyed the giant bird with some misgiving. "So you really are going to cook a turkey today?"

"Oh, for sure," Kendra said. "Everyone else made side dishes before they got here, but we elected not to cook the turkey beforehand. There's something about the smell of roasting turkey that makes a gathering feel like a holiday. Ain't so?"

"Um, yes?"

"If you're feeling overwhelmed, you're in good company," Tricia called out as she and E.A. joined them. "Kendra always does more than expected."

Kendra frowned. "*Nee,* that's not true."

"It kind of is," E.A. said. "But we love you anyway, Kendra." Turning to the coffeemaker, she grinned. "Ah, *kaffi!*"

That pronouncement seemed to work like the chiming of a bell, and Nate and Harley walked in.

Deciding to be useful, Beth found milk, sugar, and paper cups and became the unofficial barista. When the first pot was empty, she made another one on its heels, chatting with everyone about college, the breakfast, and the likelihood of Kendra's turkey turning out in the cabin's oven.

Later, she stood in line with the rest of the group and helped herself to the French toast, bacon, and some of the fruit salad that E.A. had brought from home.

Just as Will and Logan started gathering all the trash, Katie looked around the room. "Wait, where's Marie?"

"She wasn't feeling too well this morning," John said. "I told her to take her time getting out of bed."

E.A. got to her feet. "What's

wrong? Is she sick?"

John looked down at his feet. "*Nee,* just, um, a little tired. That's all. I brought her some crackers."

"Crackers? She didn't want anything more?" Kendra asked.

"*Nee,*" John replied. "She said she was still full from last night."

Thinking that his excuses didn't make much sense at all, Beth looked from one person to the next. They also looked skeptical . . . though a couple of the women were smiling too.

Kendra cleared her throat. "Well, since Marie is um, really tired, Beth, how about Nate and I take you to your cabin to get your things?"

She blinked, trying to keep up

with the sudden change of topic. "But I'm not sure where it is."

"You gave us some hints, though," Nate said. "Besides, we're going to have to find it sooner or later."

"Now that it has stopped snowing, it's a beautiful day," Kendra added. "Cool and crisp. At the very least, we'll have a nice walk."

"I'll join you too," said Tricia. "It will be fun."

Beth couldn't think of a thing to say except what was in her heart. "Thank you. I really appreciate it."

Kendra stood up. "Let's go in about an hour. I've got to get that turkey in first, *jah*?"

8

"We all went into the living room and ate on the floor.

"I had on Christmas music, and muted Christmas movies were playing on the TV. It was fun and easy, and because we hadn't gotten together in weeks, I'm afraid the eight of us ignored some of the other people for a bit.

"No one seemed to mind — except for Stephanie."

Before long, they were on their way. Marie had come out of her room, smelled bacon, and ran to the bathroom. John followed, Katie right behind.

Beth might have been the youngest person in the group, but even she had a pretty good idea about what was wrong with Marie. She sure wasn't going to be the one to say it, though!

Less than an hour later, the turkey was in the oven and the four of them were on their way.

"I'm not so sure about this," Beth admitted to Kendra, Tricia, and Nate as they started walking through the woods. "What if I get all of us lost?"

"I have an excellent sense of direction," Nate replied. "We'll be fine. There's no way we'll get lost trying to find our way back."

Kendra groaned. "Is that right, Nathan?"

"Well, I not only have a good sense of direction . . . but I also brought these," he said as he pulled a wad of torn white strips from his pocket. "I'm going to tie these on branches as we go."

Tricia chuckled. "Is that from an undershirt?"

"*Jah.* Maybe."

He was holding about twenty three-inch strips of white fabric, simple but ingenious. Thinking of all the time and worry she could have saved yesterday, Beth murmured, "I wish I would have thought of that."

"Now, don't go second-guessing yourself," Kendra said. "If you had found your way to and fro, you would still be alone. And that would have been a mighty sad thing, indeed."

"She's right," Tricia said. "We're glad you joined us."

Sometimes Beth felt like pinching herself. Never before had she been around a group of friends who lifted one another up so much. She'd had lots of good friends back in high school, but all of them had been like her . . . intent on pursuing their own dreams. This group seemed to be constantly looking out for one another.

"Hey, did I hurt your feelings?"

Kendra asked.

"Oh, no. I was just thinking of how each of you is so positive. You are this perfect group of friends."

"We're not perfect," Tricia said.

"Not at all," Nate added as he stopped to tie another strip of cloth on a tree. "We've all made our fair share of mistakes over the years. I, for one, have made quite a few."

Looking serious, Kendra nodded. "Nate is right. I tried to be English for a couple of years in my late teens. It's a long story, but I was struggling so much, I ended up in rehab."

"But you're Amish." Realizing how that sounded, Beth held up a hand. "I'm sorry."

Kendra shook her head as they

continued to walk through the trees, pausing every couple of feet. "No, no need to be sorry at all. My past is unexpected, I know it. But in other ways, I feel that my path to redemption and happiness is more inspiring. No one has a perfect life, true?"

"True."

Looking fondly at her husband, Kendra said, "Now, I am glad I went through all that I did. It made me stronger and braver. And, in some ways, more content. See, I know what it feels like to be in a very dark place. Now, even the most boring or aggravating days feel easy by comparison."

"That's why you became Amish?"

"I grew up Amish, left for a while,

then got baptized after I found my way back."

Those last words resonated with Beth. Was that what she was doing now? Attempting to find her way back to herself and her future after being lost both literally and figuratively?

Kendra had given her a lot to think about, and she was content to dwell on her words and the last couple of months while they walked in silence, the snow-covered leaves and pine needles crunching under their feet.

Emerald evergreens with thick blankets of snow on their branches nestled against the bare oaks and maples. A few squirrels scampered around, and a stray cardinal or two chirped as a lone hawk circled overhead. The air was cold and crisp, but Beth was warm enough, thanks to Marie's down coat.

As they stopped so Nate could tie another strip of cotton around a tree branch, he peered into the distance.

"When the driver was taking us to our cabin, he told us there was a group of other, even more rustic cabins to the east, about a mile out. Do you recall seeing any other cabins when you drove in?"

She'd been in such a daze, but Beth tried to recall how she'd made her way to the cabin. Suddenly she remembered a few details. "The cabin was near a really small pond that was iced over and it was within sight of two other shacks that looked to be in about the same condition as mine."

Even though she wasn't able to give much information, Nate nodded like she'd given him the exact street names. "That's *gut,* Beth. That means we're on the right track." He pointed to their right. "I could be mistaken, but it looks like the trees might thin out about fifty yards or so from here. Let's go see what we can see."

"I really appreciate the three of you doing this with me."

"Beth, you need your car and your things," Kendra said. "We can't simply leave them near an abandoned shack. Someone could steal them. Besides, you were going to have to come back eventually."

"You're right." Hoping she sounded more positive than she felt, Beth smiled. "Let's go."

Sure enough, after they'd gone that fifty yards, the trees did seem to thin out. Where before, all she could see were trees and branches and snow, now they could see quite a bit more. Off to the right was a frozen pond. Just beyond that was a wide field. Five or six deer were slowly making their way across it.

"Anything look familiar?" Tricia asked.

Had she seen that pond before? She wasn't sure. She wasn't even sure about the clearing. She'd seen more than one grouping of deer, but they could obviously have been anywhere. "Unfortunately, no."

Nate tied another piece of fabric to a tree, then started walking again. "The land rises a little farther up. Let's keep going, then."

The snow was thicker in places, which made the slight incline more difficult. Beth had to stop a few times to catch her breath. The others stopped with her, though she noticed that they didn't seem to be finding the exercise as difficult as she did. It was another reminder of how little she'd done since Joel had gotten sick.

She'd slept and cried and curled up inside herself, practically daring the rest of the world to come in. Though she knew she had nothing to feel bad about, she was coming to realize that those weeks hadn't done her any favors either. Now that she was hiking in the woods, she felt cool, clean air fill her lungs and a new hope fill her heart.

She would still be grieving. She knew that. But she was starting to see that there wasn't only one way to honor someone's life. Grief wasn't an easy task or a simple one.

Just as importantly, she knew that Joel would never have wanted her to retreat from the rest of the world in some kind of misguided effort to honor his memory.

"What do you think, Beth?" Kendra said.

"I think I need to hike more," she blurted before realizing that Kendra was looking at the horizon.

"Oh! I don't know . . . wait!" she exclaimed as she saw a red sedan. "That's my car."

"We found it! Good for you, Beth," Tricia exclaimed as she held up her fist for a bump.

Touching her fist to Tricia's, Beth's first thought was that it was so strange to be doing something like that with a woman wearing a *kapp* and bonnet. Then she was reminded of everything she'd seen during their walk and she realized the truth. Everything — good, bad, in-between — was more than it seemed. Always, always more than it seemed.

She would do good to remember that.

9

"Before even an hour had gone by, Stephanie wanted to leave. I could tell Andy was put out with her, but all he did was ask if we could go ahead and start exchanging gifts.

"We drew numbers and then picked a gift bag out of the bin. Will's present, being the biggest, was chosen first. And wouldn't you know it? Andy had gotten number one.

"Right in front of us all, he set his plate on the floor, lifted out the tissue, and then kind of yelped as Will's critters leapt toward him."

Will spoke. "The guinea pigs were really happy to be set free, you see."

"One could say that they were too happy, Will," Marie retorted.

Kendra was glad to see Beth's mood improve as they made their way over to her car. She'd never tell her, but Kendra had been plenty doubtful about how successful their journey was going to be. She'd even told Nate that morning that she was worried about the three of them getting lost in the woods.

Instead of teasing her, Nate had simply pulled out one of his older undershirts and started making strips for them to tie onto tree branches. But that was Nate now. He put her needs first and never ignored her insecurities. She, in turn, had begun to open up more and stopped hoping he would read her mind.

They'd come a long way. Now all she had to do was hope that their first Christmas as a married couple would go as well as she hoped. And that her sister Mary would show up like she'd promised.

As they continued to hike down the hill, this time with Beth and Tricia leading the way, Nate stayed by her side.

"Are you worried about the spiders?" he teased. "If so, you can stay outside."

"I do hate spiders, that's true. But I'm still thinking about Mary and Christmas."

"Everything in our home is ready for her. We've even bought the biggest ham in the state for supper. It's going to be fine."

"It's not that big, Nate. Besides, it's just as easy to brine and glaze a big ham as a small one."

"You may be right . . . but I'm just saying that it's more than enough for you, me, your sisters, and my family." He frowned. "We'll be having leftovers for weeks."

"Nate —" She stopped herself

just in time. "Oh, you. You're trying to get me spun up, aren't ya?"

The fine lines around his eyes crinkled slightly. "Maybe. But it worked, *jah*?"

"It did. So, I guess all that means you don't think I should be worrying about making a perfect meal for everyone?"

"Maybe," he replied. "It means, I'm sure everything you make will be tasty, but even if it isn't, we're still going to have a great time. Christmas is going to be wonderful, Kendra. We have each other and a whole future ahead of us. My family loves you, and I love you too. That's what matters, ain't so?"

Feeling foolish, she nodded. "*Jah*. Being all together is what matters most. I'll keep reminding myself of that."

"Good." As they stopped beside Beth's jaunty red sedan, Nate whistled low. "I'm impressed you spent a night in this place, Beth. It looks like a good wind could blow it down in a heartbeat."

"It sure sounded like it was about to." She peered in one of the windows that faced the front. "Hey, I see my computer. I guess no one's been around here since I left." She held out her key. "I'll unlock the door."

They stood to the side as Beth inserted the key, jiggled the lock, and then finally clicked open the handle. "Um, I'll be right out."

"I'll go with you," Tricia said.

"Hold on there. I'll go in with you too," Nate said. "Kendra, do you two want to wait out here for us?"

Yes. Yes, she did. But Beth had enough on her plate without worrying about their feelings or being even more of an inconvenience than she saw herself being. "No way. I want to come inside too," she said.

Nate rolled his eyes, but Beth smiled at her, which meant everything — right until she walked right into a spiderweb. "Oh!"

"They really are everywhere, Kendra," Beth said. "I didn't lie."

"No, you most certainly did not. I'll, um, wait here."

"I'll be fast. I didn't unpack much," Beth told Tricia as they walked toward the bathroom, presumably to pack up her toiletries.

Kendra sat on an arm of the couch and looked around the room. She decorated spaces for a living, but honestly, she had no idea how to make this place much better. One would have to tear the whole thing down and start from scratch, if that was even possible.

But, maybe . . . She walked to the kitchen, just to get an idea about the appliance and countertop situation. That's when she saw a FOR SALE sign on the countertop. It was for sale, and for a song too.

Immediately, she switched gears and started dreaming about making an offer on it, then remodeling the building. If she took it down to the studs, added insulation and fresh Sheetrock, why, it wouldn't be half bad. And then the Eight could have someplace to stay every now and then.

And perhaps even once a year, they could all come back here with *kinner* in their arms. The cramped space wouldn't be so bad if they were all with friends, would it?

"Uh-oh, you've got that look in your eye," Nate said.

Unable to help herself, she picked up the flyer and showed it to him. "Wouldn't this be perfect for us all?"

"I'm not so sure about that. This place is a mess."

"But what if we all went in on this together? It wouldn't be that much."

"But everyone would have to agree to it." Holding up the flyer with one hand, he gestured with the other. "Plus, this place is going to need a lot of work. Why, just these countertops and faucets alone would be a couple hundred dollars."

"But we know someone who has a hardware store and can get everything at a discount," she said, looking right at him. "And we also know someone who has a remodeling company. Harley is super handy."

"But how would we even begin to negotiate such a thing?"

"Marie works at a bank. She could help us."

He chuckled. "You have all the answers, don't you?"

"No. But I do have hope. That's what we would need the most of, don't you think?" She couldn't explain it, but all of a sudden, she knew that buying this little cabin was going to be just what they needed to ensure that they would always have a connection. As far as she was concerned, owning a piece of real estate together would guarantee they wouldn't drift apart again.

She also realized that it would mean she'd officially be a part of the Eight — something she had wanted so badly when they were all much younger.

Nate looked like he was about to

disagree, then gazed at her a long moment. "You know what? You're right. Let's take this back to everyone and talk about it tonight."

"You mean it?"

He pressed a kiss to her brow. "I mean it, Kendra. All we can do is try, right?"

Smiling up at him, she nodded. That was right. All they could do was offer it as a suggestion. If no one else wanted to buy the cabin, she wasn't going to be upset.

But if they did . . . well, wouldn't that be something?

Beth and Tricia joined them, each holding a suitcase.

"I looked in every room and am positive I got everything," Beth announced. "I'm ready to get out of here."

"Me too," Tricia said. She grimaced. "I think I walked right into at least three spiderwebs."

"What do you think, Kendra?" Nate asked. "Are you ready to leave?"

"I suppose." She wanted to make more plans, but Nate was right. They needed to do some thinking first.

Tricia looked from one to the other. "Wait, did I miss something? Kendra, you look almost sad that we're leaving."

"I'm not sad. It was just a silly conversation," Kendra replied. Turning to Beth, she said, "Let's hope your car starts and we can get out of here."

"I'm not worried about my car working, but I am a little worried about us finding our way back," Beth said as she led the way out. "It's really too bad we can't use your strips of white fabric, Nate. That would've been great."

"I was thinking the same thing," Nate joked. "Here's hoping it doesn't take us twice as long to find our way to Kendra's turkey."

10

"Pit and Pat hadn't liked being stuck in a sack, and they were scared and hungry. For some strange reason, they completely ignored the carrot that Will had placed in the bag for them."

The drive back to the cabin had been surprisingly easy. Beth wasn't sure if the reason was because it was daylight and she had a better idea of where she was, or if it was due to Kendra's and Nate's navigation skills. Likely, it was a combination. Everything was easier with friends.

That was exactly how she thought of them now. No longer were they just nice people who had gone out of their way to help someone in need; they were her friends. They were easy to get along with and had shared more about themselves than some of the girls she'd known for years. They had gone from being strangers to friends in a matter of hours instead of weeks or months, and for that, she was grateful.

When Beth parked her car in front of the cabin, everyone ran outside to greet them. It had been so cute, like they'd been gone for days instead of just two hours. When E.A., Katie, and the others started peppering Kendra, Nate, and Tricia with questions, Beth tried to slink off to the side so she wouldn't be intruding on their conversation.

But E.A. put a stop to that. She asked Beth all kinds of questions about her car and their trip. All of them were very amused about Nate using his undershirt to mark their way too.

"We should all go out and see if we can find our way there," Logan said as they walked inside. "We could make a game of it. You know, the person who spies the most white markers gets to shower first or something."

"This might sound crazy, but it sounds like fun," Marie said.

Stretching her long legs a bit, she added, "I'd love the exercise too."

"There's also another reason that I'd like everyone to go see that cabin," Kendra said as she held out a real estate flyer. "Look at this."

Marie frowned. "Are you thinking of buying that place, Kendra?"

"Kind of."

"You aren't serious, are you?" Beth asked. "The cabin is infested with spiders."

E.A. visibly shuddered. "Spiders and who knows what else!"

"Oh, it wasn't that bad. Plus, we all know that exterminators can come," Kendra said. "They'll take care of the bugs."

Beth didn't want to be the voice of doom, but she thought Kendra was making that shack seem a whole lot better than it really was. She wouldn't be surprised if there was a mouse or two living under the floorboards. "I hate to say it, but there was more wrong with that cabin than just some unwanted spiders. It needs a lot of work. It's practically unlivable."

"You're right. It is unlivable . . . as it is," Kendra said.

Katie frowned at her. "Um, what other way is there?"

"Well . . ."

"Uh-oh," John said. "Whatever you are concocting in that head of yours already sounds expensive."

"Listen, hear me out. I had an idea."

"Which is?" John asked.

"We should buy it and fix it up."

" 'We'?" Logan raised his eyebrows.

As everyone started talking even faster, Beth perched on the arm of the couch and listened to the questions and comments flying furiously across the room.

"And then do what?" Harley asked. "Make a little bit of money?"

"Nee," Kendra replied. "I think we should keep it."

"You want to own that place?" Tricia asked.

"It could be fun," Kendra protested. "We could each have a week just for ourselves."

"What about the other weeks?" Will asked. "There's fifty-two of them to worry about, you know."

Kendra's cheeks turned pink. "Well, we could also let our family and friends rent it. That would help pay for its upkeep. And then, how about we consider returning to stay all together one time a year?"

Katie looked at her husband. "What do you think, Harley? I kind of think it might be nice to have a place for all of us to use."

He scratched his chin before speaking in his usual thoughtful manner. "There's a lot of weeks in a year, that is true. And all of us have a number of siblings and extended family members. I bet Kyle and his wife, Gabby, would be real happy to stay in the cabin for a spell. I know he'd help us do repairs if he could use it."

"Of course he could use it," Nate said. "He's part of the family."

John laughed. "Honestly, if we asked all our families to help with the cabin in some way, we'd have no trouble using it year-round. My family alone could take care of a whole month."

Feeling a little wistful, Beth smiled at the group. They were now all talking over one another, playfully calling out weeks they wanted and volunteering skills they had. It was adorable.

And, if she was honest, kind of heartbreaking too. Tomorrow she would drive home and probably never see any of them again. Everything that they'd talked about and all the plans would still go on, but without her.

All she would be to them was a memory.

Katie grinned after volunteering her expertise in booking guests and arranging reservations online. "I think this might actually happen," she declared, looking like she'd just won a big prize. "I'm so glad you found it, Kendra."

"*Nee,* I only thought of the idea." Kendra looked at Beth. "Beth, here, is the person who found the cabin. If not for her, we wouldn't even be talking about such a thing."

"You're exactly right," John said. "Beth, what do you think? Are you in?"

The whole gang was looking in her direction. Feeling incredibly awkward, she tried to focus on his question. Was she in? In what? Boy, had she really zoned out for so long that she had no idea what he was asking?

"I'm sorry, I don't think I understand," she said at last. "Am I in for what?"

"To take a week," Kendra said.

"And to join us one week a year," Nate added. "That is, if you want to see us again."

"You'd want me to come?"

Marie walked over and rubbed her back. "Of course. We want you to be our friend, Beth. I promise, all of us want that."

"Really?"

"We took a secret vote last night when you were asleep," Will joked.

"It was a tough decision, but in the end we decided you're someone we want to know."

She grinned. "Gee, thanks. In that case, I'm in." And with that acceptance came a feeling of hope and warmth that she hadn't felt for far too long. Like a good friend, she'd welcomed it with open arms.

11

"Those tiny guinea pigs charged out of the sack, kind of leapt at Andy, then darted across the room. I hadn't realized they could run so fast. Or could hide so well . . . in a Christmas tree."

It was their last night together. Not just for the getaway, but also for the next couple of weeks, at the very least.

When they got home tomorrow, Marie knew everything was going to rush into high gear. She and

John would start making final plans for their own families' Christmas celebrations. John's parents were hosting a late lunch on Christmas and everyone — even Marie's parents — would bring a dish. Afterward they'd all exchange presents. Marie and John had already purchased special gifts for each other and their parents, but now, with their big announcement, she wanted to do something more.

Lying on her side of the bed while she waited for John to get out of the shower, Marie tried to think of all the cute ideas she'd seen on Pinterest, but none of those sounded right.

Maybe she could run to the big supercenter nearby and get some baby bibs or something?

"Are you going to take a nap?" John asked when he entered the room.

"No, I was just trying to think of a way to tell our families about the baby."

His expression warmed as he sat down next to her. "We *canna* just tell them and be done with it?"

"No. I want it to be memorable."

His voice softened as he kissed her temple. "Marie, it will be memorable no matter what."

"I want a keepsake or something." Looking up, she smiled at him. "My mother would love that. You know she would."

"I know if we get her something, we're gonna have to get my mother something as well."

She sat up abruptly. "I've got it. How about you draw something?"

His eyebrows lifted. "Like what? A babe?"

"No, silly. Like 'grandparents to be' or something like that. Could you do that?"

"I'll do whatever you want, Marie."

She knew he meant it too. "You really are the best husband."

"If I am, it's because I love you." His lips twitched. "When should we tell the news to all our friends?"

They thought about the logistics for a moment. "The right thing would be to wait until after Christmas. But I don't think we have plans to see everyone for a while."

"Even I know we shouldn't tell some people weeks before the others."

"Is it bad if we tell them before our families?"

"I don't think so . . . unless you think I need to draw everyone some pretty picture for tonight."

"You really think it's okay?"

"I think we can do whatever we want, Marie. Our friends will keep the secret . . . and I also think that even if they're a little hurt that they weren't informed right away, they'll get over it."

He was right. There wasn't one right way to do it. "Let's tell them tonight after we eat."

Pulling her into his arms, John murmured, "That gives us plenty of time, then."

"For what?"

"For this, Marie," he murmured just before he kissed her.

Marie had fallen asleep cuddling next to John and had only woken up when she'd heard everyone talking in the main room. After brushing her hair and splashing water on her face, Marie joined them all at last.

The moment she walked in, John looked her way. She smiled at him before walking over to all the women in the kitchen. Everyone was helping with the final preparations for their big turkey dinner.

"We're so glad you could join us at last," Katie teased.

Marie felt her cheeks heat. "Everyone, I'm so sorry. I don't know what happened. One minute I was talking to John and the next I fell asleep."

"John was adamant about you needing your rest," E.A. said. "We all understood."

"I can't believe I slept so long. He should have woken me up."

"He seemed to think it was a really good thing. Just like you only wanting crackers this morning made perfect sense," Katie said.

Marie gulped. "I guess that sounded a little odd?"

"Maybe. Actually, we weren't exactly sure what to think." Smiling at the other women, Katie murmured, "Since you fell asleep first last night, your exhaustion was a mystery, really."

"Or, perhaps, not a big mystery at all," E.A. said. She was smiling too.

Noticing the women giving one another knowing looks again, Marie felt more than a little awkward. Why, even Beth looked like she was holding back a comment. Marie felt like she should share the news about the baby, but she didn't want to do it without John.

Deciding to simply move on, Marie walked over to Kendra's side. "It certainly smells like Thanksgiving in here."

"That's because our turkey is almost done."

"I'm still amazed that big bird fit

in that little oven."

"Once we wiped down the inside, it started up just fine," Beth said. "And Kendra here went outside and pulled out a huge container of stuffing from the cooler."

Marie noticed that there was an array of dishes spread out on the countertop. Green bean casserole, smashed sweet potatoes, macaroni and cheese. "Everyone brought so much. I feel terrible that I didn't contribute more."

"We're glad you didn't," Tricia said. "Really."

Kendra was carefully spooning some drippings into a metal saucepan. "Tricia is telling the truth," she said as she got to her feet and closed the oven door.

"But still . . ."

"I made the sweet potatoes before we arrived," E.A. said.

"Beth and I made the macaroni and cheese and casserole about an hour ago," Katie said. "Beth, you are a *gut* cook."

"Thank you," Beth replied. "I can't make a lot of things, but I'm good at following directions."

Becoming even more confused, Marie said, "Was I supposed to bring a dish?"

"Nee," Kendra said quickly.

"Really?" She knew she wasn't a good cook, but she wasn't that bad. "Come on. Remember how I made that squash casserole the last time we got together?"

"I don't think any of us could ever

forget it, Marie," Tricia said as she walked into the kitchen.

Trish was sweet, and Marie feared, absolutely honest. "It was that bad?"

"Logan fed his portion to Kendra's dog, Blue," Tricia said. "I'm sorry, Marie."

"Did Blue eat everyone else's too?"

"I never got any," E.A. said. "Sorry, but I knew better."

"Fine. What can I do to help you?"

"Not a thing. Why don't you go rest and put your feet up?"

"There's no need. My feet are fine."

"Are you sure, Marie?" Tricia asked. "They're not swollen or anything?"

Tired of dancing around the subject, she blurted, "One of you, please tell me the truth. Did John tell you our news?"

"*Nee.* We've been waiting for you to tell us."

"Fine! I'm pregnant." And yes, she did sound a little grumpy about it.

All the women hugged her and started laughing.

"What's going on?"

"Marie is going to have a baby!" Tricia called out.

All the men started laughing too.

"John, did you let the cat out of the bag?"

"Nope. But I'm afraid the nap was a good sign, Marie," he said as he walked to her side.

"When is the big day? When are you due?" Katie asked.

"I'm not sure. I only just took the home test." Doing a little bit of mental math, she said, "Maybe in August or so?"

"August is a fine time to have a baby," Kendra said with a smile.

"How do you know? You aren't expecting too, are you?"

Kendra hugged her again before gazing at her with a soft smile. "Oh, Marie. Haven't you heard? *Any* time is a grand time to have a baby. It's common knowledge."

Marie smiled. "I'm excited. I haven't told my parents yet, though. We're going to give them the news on Christmas morning."

"It will be a lovely present. The best gift ever."

12

"It was very exciting. We all jumped up and tried to capture the little things. Well, all of us except for Stephanie. All she did was pick up her gift bag, stand on our couch, and announce that she wanted to leave. But Andy shook his head. He said there was no way he was leaving before we located Pit and Pat."

"You still look a little squeamish, Marie," E.A. said. "Are you sure you don't want me to do the driving this morning?"

"What a sight that would be! An Amish woman driving a black Escalade down the highway."

E.A. grinned. "It would be quite the sight, but that wouldn't matter to me. If it would help you, I would do it."

"You'd probably get a talking-to from your bishop."

"Maybe, maybe not. I have a feeling he might agree that there is a time and a place for everything. I mean, just because I joined the church doesn't mean I lost my wits. I haven't forgotten how to drive."

"Thank you for the offer, but I'm all right. Those soda crackers really helped. Honestly, I think I'm in a bit of a funk about us having to leave. I wish we could all stay here a little bit longer." Looking around the cabin, Marie realized that it now just looked worn and dated — not grubby. She was going to miss it.

Boy, they'd had a good three days here. She'd gotten to spend lots of time with John and all of their best friends. She felt like they'd reconnected again after all the turmoil and changes in their lives.

Things were different now. Many of the Eight were now in pairs. And Andy was gone. But in his place, God had given them more close friends. And in some of their cases, children.

"I bet you can't wait to see Roy and Jemima," Marie said, speaking about E.A.'s adopted children.

E.A.'s expression softened. "I can't. I've really missed them. And I can hardly wait to spend our first Christmas with them. Plus, as much as Will and I have enjoyed this little break, we haven't been able to stop thinking about those two. The last thing I'd ever want was for them to worry about us not wanting to be with them or, even worse, not coming back."

"You and Will have sure taken on a lot."

She shook her head. "*Nee.* We've been given a lot." Glancing over at Beth, who was helping Kendra carry some boxes out to their cars, she said, "Every time I've wondered why things happen, I'm reminded that it's not my job to wonder why. All I need to do is simply keep an open mind."

Marie nodded. "Well said. I'm embarrassed about how much I didn't want Beth here. But in some ways, I don't think this weekend would have been the same without her."

"I've been thinking the same thing. She's a nice person, but her grief reminded me of how far we've all come. I hope and pray that one day she'll feel about Joel like we do about Andy. We miss him but we haven't decided to honor his life by giving up either."

"Hope is a good thing," Marie said. Peeking at the clock, she realized it was already almost ten.

"Come on, everyone! Let's get organized so we can all get home."

"We're ready," Nate said. "Our driver said he's ten minutes away and that the roads are fine."

E.A. frowned. "We only have ten minutes to get all our things sorted and out of this cabin."

"We don't all have to leave at the same time, E.A.," Will reminded her.

"Sure we do," Katie said. "I don't want to leave if the rest of you are here. We Eight need to stick together — even when we're a bit more than 'eight.' "

Marie grinned at Will's facial expression. Like Will, the rest of the men seemed completely confused by Katie's statement, but like herself, the women were all smiling. Some things never changed, she guessed.

Two hours later, Marie was pulling onto Beth's street. She, John, Kendra, and Nate had elected to follow Beth home in case her parents had questions for them. The others had crammed into the driver's large van, which would drop them all off at their houses.

They'd separated with a chorus of hugs and promises that they'd see each other on New Year's Eve, if not before.

Now, as they parked right outside of Beth's house and got out of their cars, Marie noticed that Beth looked tense.

"Hey, are you all right, Beth?"

"Yes."

Kendra said, "What did your parents say when you called them?"

"They sounded both excited that I was coming home and annoyed about the trouble I've caused them. It turns out that they had heard I'd left school on Thursday. When I didn't show up or call them, they got worried. I should have thought about that."

"Perhaps if you talk to them about how you've really been feeling, they'll understand?" Marie asked.

"Maybe." Visibly steeling herself, she said, "Well, let's go get this over with."

They started walking up the driveway. "Is this your family's sleigh?" Kendra asked. She stopped and ran a hand along one of the runners.

"It's my father's. He built it."

It was a lovely sleigh, indeed, shiny and black. Someone had fastened a beautiful wreath to the front of it as well, with shiny brass sleigh bells attached to its bright red ribbon. Marie thought it was beautiful.

"That's a fine-looking sleigh," Nate said.

Beth chuckled. "If you told my father that, it would make his year. He built it himself."

"What?"

"He's always wanted to be a woodworker."

"I think he already is."

The moment they reached the walkway leading to the door, the front door opened and Beth's parents came out, along with two teenaged boys. "I didn't know you had brothers," Kendra said.

"Yeah. Richard and Evan. Seventeen and fifteen," she said. "They . . . well, they're great, if you can believe that," Beth added as she opened the door and got out.

"Elizabeth!" her mother cried before engulfing her in a hug.

"Something tells me that everything is going to be all right," John murmured.

"I was just thinking the same thing," Kendra said as she took Nate's hand to help her out.

By the time Marie joined the

group, everyone was shaking hands and introducing themselves.

"Mom, Dad, this is Marie Byler. She's John's wife."

"Nice to meet you. Thank you for helping Beth," her father said.

"I'm glad we were there. And, I have to say, we all enjoyed getting to know her. After spending two days in a cabin together, I think we're all officially friends now."

Beth blushed but looked pleased.

"Beth told me you built that sleigh, Mr. Trainor," Nate said. "It's a beauty."

"Thank you! It took me three years to fashion the wood in my workshop."

"I kept telling him that it was good enough, but he wouldn't listen," Beth's mother said. "It had to be just right."

"It's not as good as an Amish-made one, of course, but I'm really proud of it," her father added. "The boys here helped too."

"Can I take a look at it?"

"Oh, sure." Mr. Trainor walked Nate and John to the middle of the yard, chatting about pine as he did. Beth's brothers joined them. Marie figured they were probably glad to talk about something besides their sister.

That left Beth, her mom, Marie, and Kendra standing together.

"Oh, where are my manners? Would you girls like to come inside and relax for a spell? I could make a fresh pot of coffee."

"Thank you, but we're going to get on our way soon," Marie said. "As nice as the cabin was, I know we're all ready to take showers in our own homes."

Kendra giggled. "And by 'nice,' Marie is being sarcastic. The cabin wasn't all that nice at all. More like a wreck disguised as a cabin."

"It was still better than the place I spent Thursday night in," Beth said.

"I *canna* disagree with you there. It was a spider-infested mess, for sure."

"Sounds like you've got a lot to tell us, Beth," her mother said.

"I know I do. But, I promise, it's not all bad news. In spite of how my trip started out, a lot of good happened."

Looking at them all, Mrs. Trainor said, "You know, I can hardly believe Beth got so lucky to find all of you. I think I'm going to shudder every time I think about who she could have stumbled upon. Or, if she never had found shelter."

"Mom, don't think about the worst. I'm fine."

When the men joined them, John said, "I think we need to get on our way now." Holding out his hand, he said, "It was nice to meet you."

"It was nice to meet all of you. Thank you for saving our daughter."

Just as Marie was about to refute that bold declaration, Kendra replied, "You're welcome. Merry

Christmas."

After another round of goodbyes and hugs, the four of them were back in the vehicle and on their way again.

When Marie got on the highway, she said, "Kendra, why did you say 'You're welcome'? Thanking us for saving Beth was a bit dramatic, don't you think?"

"Oh, I don't know. In some ways I think we did save her."

"You really think she could have died?"

"Maybe, but I wasn't talking about the elements. I was thinking instead about how she was emotionally. Beth was in a bad place. She was out of hope and spiraling. Now, I see something in her eyes that I like."

"I saw that too," Nate said. "It was acceptance and maybe a little bit of hope."

"We gave her that," Kendra said softly. "Elizabeth needed to be reminded that life may not always be fair and that sometimes it's just really hard and painful. But that there's always another day."

"Well said, Kendra," John said.

Marie couldn't have agreed more.

13

"Stephanie's announcement made one of the guinea pigs peek out, which made several people reach for it . . . which made the tree fall down. Since Stephanie refused to move, one of the branches hit her face. Next thing you knew, Stephanie had a black eye and was yelling at everyone.

"I would have felt worse for her if I wasn't so worried about all of my mother's special spun glass ornaments."

"To be fair, all of us tried to help the girl, except for Andy," John said. "He seemed content to simply sit and hold the guinea pigs."

"They seemed mighty pleased to be there," Will said.

"Twenty minutes later, Stephanie had not only broken up with Andy, but she'd also called her mother to pick her up. After she left, not a one of us knew what to say. But instead of being upset, Andy started laughing.

" 'I'll never forget this moment,'

he said. 'This might be the best Christmas we've ever had.' "

Marie looked at everyone and smiled. "You know what? I think, in a lot of ways, Andy was right. It's one of my favorite Christmas memories. Guinea pigs, Stephanie, and all."

Christmas Day

Climbing into her bed, Beth stretched out her legs and snuggled deep into the flannel sheets that her mother had bought for her when she still had braces on her teeth. The sheets were light blue and decorated with all kinds of dancing penguins. Boy, she used to love these sheets!

Rubbing her thumb against the soft cotton, now worn to a smooth finish after so many washings, Beth smiled softly. Maybe she still did love them. They made her feel comfortable and cozy and brought back a thousand memories of simpler times. Moments when she'd climb into bed thinking about gifts she wanted to receive, friends she wanted to see, even boys she wanted to date.

Now, although she wasn't all that much older, she felt like she'd certainly moved beyond those times.

But, to her surprise, she hadn't moved past Christmas.

That was the biggest surprise of the day, she decided. For the last month, ever since she'd gone back to school after a really terrible Thanksgiving, all she'd been doing was living in dread of the next holiday. She hadn't wanted to think about celebrating Christmas without Joel. She hadn't wanted to even be reminded that she was still alive and he was gone forever.

But today? Well, although she still had a number of moments when she missed Joel, she'd had far more when she'd simply been thankful. Thankful for her brothers and her parents and the fact that her mother decorated the house exactly like she always had. She'd found comfort in familiarity. In the lop-sided artificial tree. In the cran-berry Jell-O salad that her father hated but always put on his plate to make her mother happy. In the way her brothers griped and joked and called their friends and played Xbox in the basement while she helped her mother cook.

None of it was perfect, but it was familiar. And it was another sign that time moved on even when sometimes she was sure she would not.

"Hey, Bethy?" Richard called out. "You up?"

"Yep. Come on in."

Her seventeen-year-old brother came in. As usual, he was dressed in a pair of sweatpants and one of his many high school sports T-shirts.

"What's up?"

"Hmm? Oh, nothing." He stopped at the edge of her bed. His hair was damp. He must have taken a shower right after they'd all gone upstairs.

"Sure about that?" He didn't usually wander into her room, not since he was in elementary school, anyway.

After glancing at her sheets, he smiled and sat down on the bottom corner of her mattress. "Um, I was just thinking about you and . . ."

"Joel."

"Yeah."

"What about us?"

"Well, you don't seem as sad. I guess we all thought you were going to spend Christmas like you did

Thanksgiving."

"Crying and moping and generally being miserable?"

"Um, well, yeah." He looked down at the sheets, then lifted his head again. "I guess you're feeling better?"

"I am. When I was lost in the woods and then found again — and then stuck in that cabin with all those people — we talked a lot." She paused, trying to find the right words to describe their story. "Richard, it was the craziest thing. They're all really different, but they've been friends forever. Some of them used to even call themselves the Eight."

"Sounds weird."

"I thought so too, until they

started telling me about how close they all were. And how their unofficial leader was a guy named Andy. He died about two years ago. His death was sudden and unexpected. They were crushed."

"Wow."

"Yeah. I guess hearing how honest they were about their pain and the things they went through made me realize that I wasn't the only one who had experienced loss."

"So, talking about Joel helped you heal?"

"It did. But what helped the most was what one of them said. She was talking about mourning Andy and feeling hopeless, but then events and new people and experiences came into their lives that made her look at everything in a whole new way. She said that even in the darkest of moments, light can shine if one bothers to notice it."

"Bothers?"

She nodded. "She said something about how it's easy to be so blinded by worries or pain that a person forgets to notice flowers blooming or babies crying or a good book or a smile from a friend . . . or even the miracle of Christmas Day."

"Wow."

"Yeah. And that's when I realized something else: no matter how bad something is, it doesn't have to be that way the next day. That there is always, *always* the promise of tomorrow. And that promise, even when it isn't Christmas or something special, or even something all that good? Well, it made me feel better. It started making me feel whole again."

Richard got up. "I'm glad. I . . . well, I've missed you, Bethy."

"I missed you too. But I'm here now. I'm back."

"Merry Christmas," he said as he edged to the door.

"Merry Christmas, Rick," she said as he walked out into the hall.

Turning off the light, she laid down again, closed her eyes, and thought about Joel and the friends she'd made.

And then she realized for the first time in quite a while that she was eager for the morning to come.

ABOUT THE AUTHOR

A practicing Lutheran, **Shelley Shepard Gray** is the *New York Times* and *USA Today* bestselling author of more than eighty novels, which have been translated into multiple languages. During her years of researching the Amish community, she has depended on her Amish friends for gossip, advice, and cinnamon rolls. She lives in Colorado with her family and writes full-time.

The OLDEST ENIGMA OF HUMANITY

The OLDEST ENIGMA OF HUMANITY

THE KEY TO THE MYSTERY OF THE PALEOLITHIC CAVE PAINTINGS

BERTRAND DAVID

AND

JEAN-JACQUES LEFRÈRE

TRANSLATED BY MOLLY GROGAN LYNCH

Arcade Publishing • New York

Arcade Publishing books may be purchased in bulk at special discounts
for sales promotion, corporate gifts, fund-raising, or educational purposes. Special editions can also be created to specifications. For details,
contact the Special Sales Department, Arcade Publishing, 307 West
36th Street, 11th Floor, New York, NY 10018 or
arcade@skyhorsepublishing.com.

Visit our website at www.arcadepub.com.

10 9 8 7 6 5 4 3 2

Library of Congress Cataloging-in-Publication Data is available on file.
ISBN: 978-1-62872-321-2

Printed in the United States of America

I

Drawing has always been a passion of mine. When I was six or seven years old, I spent all my free time inventing elaborate stories that I illustrated carefully with colored markers. I took my cues for these from the adventures of Lucky Luke, an unlikely cowboy hero in a checkered shirt forever pursuing evildoers intent on harming a tribe of Indians. My family was greatly amused by my first sketches. Although I wasn't particularly talented, their enthusiasm, forced as it was, spurred me on. Evenings and vacations, right up to adolescence, I could always be found with my No. 2 pencils, my erasers, and my colored pens. Eventually, like many an aspiring illustrator, I had to acknowledge, with no little disappointment, that an inseparable gulf yawned between my efforts and the talent of the famed comic strip authors I so admired. Nevertheless, fortune did smile on me once, when I had the opportunity to meet one of the greatest of these, André Chéret, who responded patiently to my questions during an interview I recorded. This was in 1975, and his character, Rahan, known as the "son of a savage era," was the hero of boys my age. The illustrations were realistic, executed with great flourish, and the stories told of the most thrilling adventures of this Cro-Magnon man, who was also a stunning example of the finest moral and physical qualities and who never surrendered to his adversaries, neither the hostile environment nor the hordes of disgracefully organized tribes, which were often under the sway of sorcerers with the most obscurantist ideas. They always lost. Sometimes, by some magical time-bending, Rahan crossed paths with a Jurassic dinosaur; evidently, the scenario's author, Roger Lécureux was not averse to taking liberties with prehistoric history. This detracted nothing from Rahan's appeal for his audience, who also came to appreciate through his exploits something of the harshness of life for the first generations of humanity.

In all honesty, however, my interview left me with a lingering despair, as it brought me face to face with the virtuosity of which only exceptional illustrators are capable; with just a few, quick strokes of India ink from his sable brush, he could bring to life an impeccably proportioned, perfectly muscled Rahan, who acknowledged our awed gaze with a short wave of his hand from across the freshly killed tiger at his feet. Chéret modestly assured me that his mastery was no accident: he himself had toiled daily at his drawing for twenty years and I should go back to the basics—everything could be learned with time and patience. Emboldened by this frank lesson, I continued to draw for years. All the same, one day, my admiration for comic strip illustrators was stopped short by a totally new idea: the real geniuses of drawing filled the pages of any art history encyclopedia. And so it was, with the discovery of the drawings of Delacroix, thanks to a gift I received on my fifteenth birthday, that a new passion began for me. The sensitivity, the evocative power of his sketches, confirmed for me what I had already suspected: there are as many ways of drawing as there are illustrators—even for those who render their subjects realistically—and that any sketch with an ounce of imagination always reflects the personality of its artist.

Big, fat volumes on art history soon replaced the comic books on my shelves, and I put together a little painting museum of my own invention by cutting out all the art photos I could find in magazines. This was long before Google Images, and it may be hard today to fathom the joy I felt discovering a Rembrandt I had never before seen in a Catholic magazine I had swiped from my aunt. I gravitated towards monographs that spanned the entire career of a single artist, including his earliest works. I probably wanted to convince myself that even the greatest talents had to struggle for years at their craft, making gradual progress before coming fully into possession of their art. I remember two youthful self-portraits in particular: one—mostly unsuccessful—painted by Géricault moved me, while the the perfection of another, done by Ingrès when he was only twenty years old, left me stupefied (I learned later that he had entirely reworked the portrait when he was in his seventies). I moved on to the biographies of famous artists, which I read one after the other, only to learn yet again that, with the notable exception of Picasso and Dürer perhaps, the rest had sweated at their drawing tables for many long years before developing both mastery and style. I read, too, that, during the Italian Renaissance, a student was required to sketch for seven years before ever picking up a paintbrush, "never abandoning his study of drawing for even a Sunday or a holiday." Aspiring painters sometimes became apprentices at the age of twelve: plenty of time to become a recognized master at the age of twenty, as Raphaël did.

My reading led me to yet more books, so that I became familiar with a large swath of Western painting and its history. As much as I was amazed by the great leap forward made in the sixteenth century, with the discovery of perspective, I was frustrated by the dearth of surviving paintings from Antiquity, whose artists, if Pliny the Elder is to be believed, were more famous than even athletes and generals. There was only one chapter in my weighty *Art History in Two Volumes*, published by the Encyclopedia Quillet, that did not enchant me, and this was the chapter on prehistoric cave paintings.

Most explanations that accompanied the requisite photographs of the bulls at Lascaux dwelled on their beauty
and elegance, but said little more. Somehow, subconsciously, these images bothered me; despite their artistry
and fame, they seemed to me somehow cold and unreal,
as if a fog separated them from me, or as if I couldn't see
them as they were meant to be seen. Only recently did
I begin to understand why.

II

I have now been drawing and painting for more than thirty years. Following studies at the Ecole des Beaux-Arts in Rennes and ten more years as a graphic artist, I work semi-professionally as a painter and illustrator. Many of my leisure hours have been devoted to studying the history of painting and drawing. I also draw somewhat fantastical comic strips on subjects having to do with archeology, so I spend much time researching a variety of subjects. While searching for new ideas for these stories, I came back to the prehistoric paintings in the caves at Lascaux and Altamira, still as mysterious on one side of the Franco-Spanish border as they are on the other. One possible response, which I had never taken the time to investigate, had come to me several years earlier while I was tucking my son into bed. This was in 2004, and my future heir was eight years old. I was about to kiss him goodnight, and we were confiding a few last words to each other before turning off the light. I happened to glance around at the mess in his room and I looked for a moment at the opposite wall. A far-fetched idea crossed my mind: what if that was the solution? Impossible, I thought. Too simple. I turned off the light and didn't think of it again.

At the most, I had perhaps discovered an idea for a comic strip. I still was as much in the dark as before regarding prehistoric painting, even though the relatively recent discovery of the caves at Chauvet and Cosquer had given rise to a number of articles and fascinating documentaries, as well as the publication of some magnificently illustrated coffee table books, the kind one pages through slowly on Christmas Day, places carefully on a shelf, and never reads again. So it was that I picked up once again these venerable books, some of which were rather scientific. They soon had me marveling again over the work of these prodigious artists: the beauty and refinement of the drawings and paintings, their grasp of realism, the pureness and the assuredness of the line. I noticed as well that the science devoted to parietal art did not stretch very far back. At one time, in fact, the authenticity of these paintings had been cast into doubt.

III

In the summer of 1879, a Spaniard named Marcelino Sanz de Sautuola was exploring a cave that had been discovered recently on his land in Santillana del Mar, near Santander in Cantabria. His daughter, Maria, who was along that day, spied the bulls painted on the high ceiling: "Papa, mira, toros pintados!" The following year, Sanz de Sautuola published his discovery, which called into question much of what was known about prehistory. The scientific community appeared skeptical, even contemptuous of his conclusions, refusing to allow that such realistic paintings as were found in the Altamira caves could be so old. Their vividness and their perfect state of conservation argued for more recent, perhaps medieval, origins. That prehistoric man, those primitives, could have produced images as beautiful as these seemed highly improbable. Specialists like Gabriel de Mortillet and Emile Cartailhac smelled a fraud. As the controversy faded, the incident was soon forgotten.

It would take almost twenty years for the authenticity of that prehistoric art to be recognized internationally by academics and scholars. More discoveries revealed yet more drawings, at the caves known as La Mouthe (1895), Font de Gaume, and Combarelles (1901), in the Dordogne in southwest France. Some of these drawings were veiled by a thin film of calcite, a sure sign of considerable age. With so many similar images in sites far removed from one other, any accusations of fraud no longer held water. One of the staunchest opponents of Altamira's veracity, Emile Cartailhac, published a thundering article in the journal *L'Anthropologie*, titled "The Altamira Cave: Confessions of a Skeptic." The article's reverberations would be felt around the world, bestowing official status at last on prehistoric cave art.

Still more discoveries followed, in Spain (La Clothilde, in Cantabria, 1906) and in France: Niaux (1906), Tuc d'Audoubert (1912), and Les Trois-Frères (1914), all located in the mountainous Ariège region of southwest France. The Lascaux site in France's Périgord *département* would be uncovered considerably later in 1940. Destined to become the most famous of all the caves, as both an enduring symbol and a high temple of prehistory, it was inscribed on the French National Register of Historic Monuments only days after its discovery. Still more caves and paintings were found, often by pure chance, by people with no interest at all in archeology or prehistory. The boom in speleology, post-World War II, was largely responsible for this. One of the most extraordinary discoveries of all happened in 1991: the Cosquer cave at Cap Morgiou, near Marseille, which can only be reached through a 175-meter-long tunnel that lies 40 meters below the surface of the Mediterranean. The rise in sea levels occurring over the last millennia explains its hidden entrance, which makes Cosquer the only site of parietal art that lies underwater.

Today, no fewer than 250 painted caves dating from the Palaeolithic Period, or Old Stone Age, have been recorded in Europe. The majority of these are located in southwest France or northern Spain, but a few more sites have been discovered in Italy and England.

In all the history of the study of these caves, two names must be mentioned. The first, and the most famous, is the Abbé Henri Breuil (1877–1961), otherwise known as the "Pope of Prehistory." Never a practicing priest, Breuil was appointed the first chair in Prehistory at the Collège de France, a position created specifically for him in 1929. The second name to remember is that of the anthropologist and prehistorian André Leroi-Gourhan (1911–1986), who was named to the same chair in 1969. After lengthy study of the wall paintings of the Upper Paleolithic Period, he developed a theory according to which this particular art form follows an "evolving trajectory, the longest ever recorded in art, from 30,000 BC to 8,000 BC." By comparing styles,

Leroi-Gourhan theorized four stages of Paleolithic cave paintings, moving from a beginning phase of rough traces of lines to a final phase of complex, and above all, realistic, images in a gestational process spanning several millennia. This theory prevailed in the field for many decades before being overturned suddenly in 1994 by the discovery of Chauvet at Vallon-Pont d'Arc in the Ardèche canyons. Considered the oldest known cave of its kind in the world, it contains, paradoxically, the most realistic and the most accomplished paintings yet discovered. Chauvet suggests that when prehistoric man first set out to draw animals, he did it perfectly, right from the start, and continued to do so with the same mastery for millennia. The equivalent, in modern terms, would be to assert that from the year 200 AD to our twenty-first century, art has undergone no appreciable evolution.

The Chauvet cave demonstrates that beginning already in the Aurignacian age, which is the oldest tool culture of the Upper Paleolithic Period, prehistoric man was painting animals with perfect skill. In other words, cave art did not undergo a gradual evolution toward naturalism because naturalism was, in fact, the point at which it began. This contradicted entirely all the chronological theories already in place at the time, including those of Leroi-Gourhan and his followers, whose belief in a stylistic progression has now been definitively abandoned.

IV

I attempted to learn more by studying the texts I had to hand which treat the various studies undertaken of the caves, but my efforts left me feeling perplexed. All these books faithfully reproduced every item of data known and recorded, but none approached the question that all of these studies seemed to beg when looking at these paintings, some of which are more than twenty-thousand years old: *what do they mean?*

This line of interrogation, among many others, gradually surfaced as I continued my studies, but eluded my attempts to answer it. After a while, with a determination that would have made both Indiana Jones and Sherlock Holmes envious, I decided to draw up a list of all the questions I could think of. The first of these focused naturally on what the paintings meant and what function they might serve. Why paint animals, and why on the same wall, and why sometimes were these images large while other times they were small? Why were they in such remote places and so difficult to reach? Why were these particular species of animals drawn when they were not the animals that prehistoric man most often hunted? Why do the animals never appear ugly or frightening or ridiculous? Why were the paintings never disfigured in any way, over so many thousands of years? Why are humans almost never depicted, nor for that matter any kind of object at all, or flora, or landscape, or dwelling? Why also, when these artists certainly seemed to know how to paint, did they never paint anything but animals?

Another line of questioning, more technical this time, was raised by the strange style of the paintings, which resemble nothing else known in art. How were the artists trained? Why did they always choose to depict the animals in profile? Why are the paintings often superimposed and how were the artists able to execute them so flawlessly, one on top of the other? Why are there no poorly drawn images, while there are many unfinished ones? Why do most of the animals resemble each other so closely? Why is it that the artists never seemed to have any difficulty painting on the uneven surfaces of the caves? What explanation can there be for the fact that certain silhouettes are composed of pigment only, with no outline, yet are perfectly recognizable?

Some more general particularities confirmed—if such a thing was ever necessary—the complexity of the mystery to be resolved. Why, in a single cave, are there paintings from many periods that are far distant from each other? What explains the stylistic consistency of the paintings, over twenty-five thousand years? Why did the artists of the Upper Paleolithic Period never work in the rooms of the caves closest to the entrances, but always in those furthest removed from them? Why are there sometimes hand stencils[1] in the same places? What is the meaning of the abstract engravings found on the cave walls? What function could such a long-lasting tradition have, and why did it end so suddenly, before any ancient text could make mention of it, like a legend lost forever to the mists of time? And how, in a long-ago age, did such a conceptual practice as painting begin?

To these, as well as the innumerable questions that remain to be asked, science seemed to have only one answer: "We don't know." The rare explanations put forth remained evasive and careful or, on the other hand, quite unfounded. With no other place to turn, and with nothing to lose, I decided to satisfy two desires at the same time, by examining the problem in its entirety but in the form of a new comic book scenario. It occurred to me that my experiences as an illustrator, rather than

---

[1] Unlike a handprint, which would be made by painting the hand with a pigment such as red ochre and applying it to the rock, a hand stencil is created by placing a hand on the rock and then blowing the pigment onto it. Upon removal of the hand, an outline of its shape remains.

a prehistorian, afforded me a different perspective on the subject. It should be noted that whereas texts on the Lascaux paintings were usually found on the Art History shelves of libraries and bookstores, the discovery of Chauvet moved them to the Science section, where they mingled with books on paleoanthropology. Whether this reversal demonstrates a certain embarrassment on the part of researchers or their uncertainty as to the domain—art or archeology—that the paintings fall under, if ever proof was needed that some subjects are poorly defined from the outset, one need look no further than parietal art.

Be that as it may, paleoanthropologists and art historians have one thing in common: they are rarely illustrators or painters. In that light, it no longer seemed far-fetched that I could join the discussion on a prehistoric mystery. My goal would be to imagine myself as a prehistoric artist in the hope of understanding his technique and intentions. Moreover, and unlike most studies undertaken up until then, my objective would be not to examine the specificities of one cave or another, but to attempt to answer the many questions on my list. To be considered valid, any hypothesis I might arrive at would have to be demonstrated using as many cases as possible: if I was going to throw myself into one of the oldest enigmas in the history of mankind, I was determined to elucidate it generally rather than get mired down in its exceptions.

I began by becoming better acquainted with all the theories ever formulated regarding the nature and function of the paintings, which would also help me avoid well-trodden ground and the disappointment of finding, after expending much time and energy, that any possible conclusions I had arrived at had already been the standard fare of specialists, or worse, disproven by them. The discovery of Altamira seemed, in fact, to have unleashed many interpretations of parietal art.

One of the oldest theories was that the paintings were purely decorative. According to this interpretation, which had the merit of being romantic at least, art was born in the caves of our earliest ancestors when *Homo sapiens* began to develop an aesthetic sense and attempted to express artistically what he found to be beautiful.

Abbé Breuil, on the other hand, believed that the caves were the site of purposeful magic rituals: by drawing the animals, prehistoric man was seeking to gain power over them, using spells to dominate the game he needed to hunt in order to survive.[2] The bison were drawn as symbols before being hunted and eaten.

Later, when several footprints of children were discovered in the clay soil of one cave, the theory was advanced that these hidden places had been the site

---

[2] Henri Breuil. *Quatre cents siècles d'art pariétal*, Montignac, 1952.

of initiation ceremonies transforming young men into hunters.

André Leroi-Gourhan applied statistical tools to the kinds of animals painted and their positions in each cave and concluded that a complex, coherent organization governed them and that this represented a long-forgotten mythological structure. Dismissing the idea that the paintings were "an anarchic agglomeration of figures from all the ages of prehistory, thrown haphazardly up onto the walls,"[3] he constructed a structuralist argument asserting that the images were, in fact, perfectly organized. He added a curious theory about pairs, positing that a male-female duality was present in the "statistical couple" formed by a horse (male) and a bison (female).

One of the best known specialists is Jean Clottes, who has spent years defending his theory of shamanism, according to which prehistoric man was attempting to channel the spirits of the animals. Clottes believes that bison, horses, and deer were the inhabitants of a ritualistic universe and that hallucinatory visions of these appeared to sorcerers in a trance-like state. He pointed to the curious postures that some animals assume in the paintings, lying on their backs, legs in the air, or seeming to ascend or descend as if on an incline, as well as the fact that the animals appear to happily share the

---

[3] André Leroi-Gourhan. *Les Religions de la Préhistoire.* PUF, 1964, p. 92.

same imaginary landscape, each cavorting in blissful ignorance of his neighbors something that could not reasonably happen in reality.

Reviewing the literature, I began to wonder if there remained any hypothesis left to be examined, any stone at all left unturned. Everyone had their theory, from totemism and cults of animal divinities, to metaphysical conceptualizations of the prehistoric world and creation myths where aspects of the paintings corresponded to the constellations as they would have appeared in the Paleolithic Period, the images constituting a veritable "map of the heavens."

A few of my questions were answered by these "explanations," but none of these approached the matter that puzzled me more than the meaning of the paintings: how were they made? Most specialists agreed that the artists drew very well and that some were even particularly talented, but that was the gist of their thinking on the subject. I remembered Chéret's lesson: artists who are generally recognized as gifted are the ones who have spent the most time working at their art. It may be true that natural talent predisposes certain illustrators to progress more rapidly than others, but no child is innately equipped with the science of drawing realistically. If a single case existed, it would have to be a complete exception, the rarest of phenomena. Since it was foolhardy to believe that all the many artists responsible for all the cave art were all exceptions, the only conclusion possible was that they learned to paint, by some means or another. But it seemed just as impossible to conceive, from what is known of prehistoric life, that these artists had the leisure time to paint or even the possibility of teaching something so complex over so many millennia.

V

The first problem to be resolved involved the sheer span of time over which the paintings were made. In 2012, new studies confirmed that the Chauvet cave was painted in approximately 32,000 BC. Radiometric dating has approximated that Lascaux is only seventeen thousand years old. It may be hard to grasp as dizzying a chronology as that, but one fact stands out: Chauvet is as old compared to Lascaux as Lascaux is to us today.

Such simple terms highlight the impressive timespan of parietal art. Another significant aspect remains to be elucidated, however; as removed from each other in time as the two caves are, their paintings are remarkably alike: the same animal motifs arranged from similar angles; the same apparently haphazard arrangement; the same inexplicable superpositions; the same "stylistic conventions." Yet, a full fifteen thousand years (fifteen thousand!) separate the artists who worked in these caves. Without a doubt, a tradition and a practice of painting were handed down over at least fifteen millennia, without undergoing any substantial modification. This would imply, logically, that a certain type of painting obeying fixed stylistic criteria was taught over the same period. A number of specialists were greatly surprised by the uniformity—we might even say, standardization—of the Paleolithic cave paintings: "One might go so far as to admit the idea that the same themes were reproduced over thousands of years, but not that the same, minor conventions were followed to draw a rhinoceros ear or a bison head."[4]

In fact, the paintings provide the only known example of a skill that has no practical use for daily survival (such as building a fire or carving arrow heads or fashioning a bow) being passed down from generation to generation over such a long period of time. Since no other paintings have been found on any other continent—which would attest to an instinctive desire in all mankind, a creative gesture common throughout humanity—it would be risky to imagine that this tradition of painting was lost for a time and then rediscovered millennia later. On the contrary, these images must demonstrate the presence of a savoir-faire that was handed down over an exceptionally long period, without interruption or significant variation. As for

---

[4] Jean Clottes, *La Gortte Chauvet. L'art des origines.* Seuil, 2010, p. 195.

any alleged symbolic significance of the paintings, as theorized by Leroi-Gourhan, this hypothesis, too, is difficult to defend: it would not have taken much—several cycles of poor harvests and low food reserves, a few particularly rigorous winters—to interrupt the practice of painting and its teaching, especially if these were reserved for only the initiated few.

In fact, in the whole history of mankind, not a single civilization, from the legendary Egyptian and Roman empires to the builders of the pre-Colombian cities, has been immune to a chance event—either natural or accidental—capable of wiping it off the map. Would we dare argue that the wealth of information we possess today might still be of interest in another 150 centuries? Yet that is precisely what the prehistoric authors of this cave art have managed to pull off despite the crude conditions of their existence. Certainly, the men and women of the Upper Paleolithic Period measured time much differently than we do today; the notion of progress was probably unknown to them. Besides the fundamental techniques required to paint so assuredly over so many years, the meaning of the images—ritualistic? symbolic? functional?—undoubtedly obeyed a complex logic that, moreover, has withstood the test of time. In that case, whatever the intended meaning of the paintings may be, it was probably not a secret that only the initiated could share. The answer to the question more likely lies in a practice of painting that was accessible to all and that was probably necessary to all, over all the vast periods beginning with the oldest cave, Chauvet, and ending with the most recent, Altamira, whose drawings date back "only" some ten thousand years BC.

VI

As improbable as the existence of a special class of Paleolithic artists seems, since there are paintings, there must have been painters. What, then, do we mean when we refer to these individuals? Let's begin by abandoning a few preconceptions about supernatural talent or mystical powers and remember what is at issue: realistic representations of the real world of the artists. Drawing is so central to human existence that we tend to think of it as an extension of nature itself: a vanity that nevertheless holds some truth. Don't blueprints often prefigure prototypes? From objects like furniture and weapons, to plans of all sorts, be they for military or business purposes, the design precedes and prepares the intention.

It may be that we no longer conceive of drawing as a cultural act presupposing the capacity for abstraction. The rendering into two dimensions of a reality experienced in three requires a kind of mental gymnastics that does not come naturally. There are, for example, native peoples living in the Amazon Basin who are unable to distinguish anything when shown a photograph: motionless, depthless images formed by pigments on paper correspond to nothing that is real for them.

Consider, moreover, an outline, a silhouette; interpreting it surpasses the natural ability of anyone who has never before been confronted with this kind of codified image, for the simple reason that our optical vision perceives colors, textures, depth, movement, shapes, and other features. "Seeing" a certain shape in a single black line (a line which does not, of course, encircle that shape in reality) without any hint of the context in which the shape might be found, is a challenge for the untrained mind. Even babies are capable of doing this, however; the human brain adapts itself to the constraints of its cultural environment. That said, this leap requires more learning than we might imagine. After all, any mammal endowed with the same powers of perception as humans remains indifferent when shown a drawing or a photograph of a predator, because a real predator only exists in three dimensions. We're not even sure that an animal perceives anything more in a photograph than colored splotches on a page.

Apparently, humans living in the Upper Paleolithic Period not only possessed this decoding ability—which other peoples did not acquire until much later—but, even more surprising, they were able to derive from it the skilled means of expression that strike us as so disconcerting today. If all civilizations developed a more or less abstract system of signs as a mnemonic tool, few primitive populations chose to draw—and to only use drawing—to represent their world, and even fewer had an understanding of anatomy and proportion, as the Paleolithic artists somehow did, over a period of twenty-five thousand years. Certainly, one of the most arresting aspects of cave art is that humans who probably never attempted to formalize their understanding of proportion by taking measurements of the animals they hunted and killed, were skilled, nevertheless, at realistic drawing, by which I mean drawing that respects both the correct proportions of the different parts of a given shape, as well as the anatomical structure of the animal being drawn.

A word or two more should be said about what I mean by "realistic" art. Around the age of four, all humans begin to draw, or at least have an understanding of what it is to draw, and, at that stage, they adopt the same code: two dots for eyes, a line for the mouth, with the memory and the imagination of the viewer supplying the rest. Later, and often into adulthood, the primary consideration of the young artist will be that his drawing conforms not to what he sees, but to what he perceives as real. It follows, when he draws, that all hands must have five fingers, all cars must have four tires, etc., even though, in the example of a car, very few angles of vision allow one to see all four tires at once.

We often forget that realism is never the first stage of drawing or painting. If we look at art through the centuries, we see clearly that realism is a more advanced stage of a process that evolves from an initial, pre-existing form, and that not all civilizations that master drawing ever arrive at that stage. In other words, it is harder to faithfully represent reality than not to. In tribal art from Africa to Latin America to the Pacific, realism is never the first option but always the last. In fact, tribal artists use more expressive codes of representation: simple orbits for eyes, unnatural proportions, and the like. I asked the illustrator Boulet why this might be and he wrote back to me in December 2011: "Imagine that future archeologists found a drawing of Astérix. What would they think of his monstrous face, with its huge nose, his ears that stick out at an atrocious angle, and that pair of close-set eyes which seem to peek out from the top of his minuscule skull? Would they think that the artist was drawing an actual, horrible midget?"

The vast majority of "primitive" or archaic art approaches the world through what we would call a "cognitive" approach: the artist draws the world as it is. In a realist or what might more properly be termed a "retinistic" approach, however, objects come into focus in the eye of the viewer. An Aztec drawing or a medieval woodcarving represents shapes in such a way that reveals what the things *are*, not how one *sees* them. The artists of both the drawing and the woodcarving make decisions: to emphasize some shapes more than others, to vary the proportions of any of the composition's elements, etc., with a single goal in mind: to tell a story with a minimum of effort and to deliver a clear message about that story. Neither artist is attempting to deliver a faithful representation of reality such as the eye perceives it.

It wasn't until the Renaissance, when Humanism placed man at the center of the natural world, that the revolutionary notion of perspective and point of view was established. At last, it was understood that shapes appear differently depending on one's location when looking at them and the direction of one's position in relation to the horizon. Perspective would forever make it possible for the illustrator to observe something from a given vantage point, to respect the proportions of each of its elements, and to situate these in their environment, according to the rules of visual reality. This being the case, we could imagine that a Renaissance artist working in a realistic approach would have to undergo a long and fastidious process of unlearning everything he thought he knew of the physical world in order to replace it with an interpretation of that world based on his visual perception of it. Any illustrator first begins by subconsciously emphasizing the proportions of those elements of his subject that seem most important. But a good realistic illustrator is able to ignore what is accidental or superfluous and focus only on the essential outlines, both interior and exterior. He may also choose to reproduce—or not—the colors and materials of the original, but he will never give one precedence over another and will always respect the proportions of what he is drawing. It goes without saying that, without a model to work from, such an artist must also possess a formidable memory for anatomy and for how volumes appear in space and combine into complex structures (which is, precisely, what the aspiring painters of the Italian Renaissance learned during those seven years of apprenticeship in pure drawing).

Of course, there have always been exceptions, virtuoso painters who never studied overmuch, but it soon becomes apparent that their work—which often borrows stylistically from other artists—is little more than what, in studio terms, used to be called "le chic," or the simple reproduction of memorized shapes of which there are a limited number of variations. Today, we are confronted by so many images, due undoubtedly to the power of the photographic image, that the very idea of realistic representation seems self-evident. This was not always the case, however; in fact, this is an extremely recent phenomenon in the history of humanity that came about only through a very long and intellectualized process of reflection.

How much more surprising then that the people who decorated the caves had already overcome this major obstacle. Their paintings are clearly the expression of an undeniable—and no less inexplicable—mastery of proportion and anatomical representation, which they arrived at without the use of any code or any theoretical conceptualization of objects, but with an economy of means that only the most recent painters and illustrators have achieved.

Be that as it may, what appeals to us most in these millennia-old paintings is what they capture of our modern world: over thirty thousand years ago, these artists cut straight to the heart of the matter by suddenly applying an approach that it has taken us centuries to master, an approach almost exclusively *retinistic*. This suggests they must have developed a procedure that owed more to optical laws than to notions of art.

After all, it makes little sense to insist that, for millennia, young illustrators learned how to paint to reproduce the same practices of their elders with absolute accuracy and without changing a hair. Why imagine that there was once an uninterrupted succession of teachers and pupils applying themselves to the acquisition, mastery, and teaching of a highly specialized craft while—as if by some miracle—also ensuring a uniformity of style over a geographical zone some thousands of kilometers wide?[5] With all due respect to our ancestors,

---

[5] Emmanuel Guy, "Esthétique et préhistoire: pour une anthropologie de style," L'Homme 165 (January–March, 2003).

and given the material conditions of life for a prehistoric hunter-gatherer, his would be rather difficult to
allow. Even if it were possible, it still wouldn't resolve
the question of the rare sites that have survived: could
twenty-five thousand years of illustrators leave so few
paintings? The authors of the *Dictionnaire de Lascaux*
made this pronouncement: "Not a single sketchbook
has survived from the Paleolithic Period, carved into a
stone, for example. The paintings must be mere copies of other artists' work." The passage of time and the
absence of any surviving examples of the tools the artists used make it difficult to understand what they were
doing or how they did it, but it does seem curious that
the majority of engravings dating from the same period,
even ones of the same animal figures as are found in the
caves, are of much poorer quality than the paintings.
Are we to conclude that the best artists were assigned to
painting and that they in turn never lowered themselves
to engrave so much as a reindeer's antler? Or that it was
only in the dark recesses of the caves that they could
fully exploit their talents, far from the gaze of others?

VIII

Judging only from the facts that have been established—those paintings that have survived in good condition and that radiometric dating has authenticated beyond any doubt—all the evidence seems to indicate that illustrators who would be considered exceptionally talented by our own standards were trained and were active over a period of at least twenty-five thousand years. That's a minimum estimate, moreover; we know nothing at all of the millennia that preceded the Chauvet paintings, whose level of mastery we find so astonishing today and whose pictorial technique is anything but hesitant. Perhaps one day the discovery of even older paintings will provide further clues about these artists' savoir-faire or add further details about the earliest beginnings of this practice.

The technical skill and the ways of representing reality that the artists passed down from generation to generation are certainly proof of a vastly rich knowledge that closely resembles our own representational approaches, a fact we may no longer fully recognize. We must conclude that not a single, destructive calamity—no famine, no war, no act of vandalism, no epidemic, no change in mentalities—ever threatened the teaching of this art over many millennia. Research in prehistory has shed more light on the Upper Paleolithic Period and its inhabitants: the population was small, possessed few tools, had a short life expectancy, was under threat by all kinds of dangers, and had to brave, at times, a much more rigorous climate than the one we know today in the same parts of the world. Compare all that with our own civilization: although we have the evident advantage of possessing written languages for recording knowledge, we have proven incapable of preserving the least tradition for more than three thousand years (we can no longer even read the French that our ancestors wrote, barely five hundred years ago). In that light, again, it seems all the more improbable that prehistoric artists could do what we cannot and passed down their secret craft for centuries, even millennia. It would be more rational by far to look for an answer in the paintings themselves, submitting them to careful observation, noting similarities across all the sites, and paying careful attention to what is clearly repeated even over a gap of seventeen thousand years (in other words, similarities in the paintings both at Chauvet and at Lascaux). What might, at first, seem anecdotal or not immediately significant would certainly take on much greater importance if it were found in these two caves, which so many years separate.

I went back to my big art books. One of the first things that stands out from the innumerable images of animals in the caves is the immense variety of sizes (figure 1). Some are several meters long (the largest, in the Hall of the Bulls at Lascaux, measures five meters in length), while others are only a few dozen centimeters big. These variations in size seem not to have been dictated by the space the artists were working in; tiny horses share a single wall with colossal buffalo, while midget mammoths run next to giant stags. Even in those cases where radiometric dating has determined that the animals in a single cave were painted several thousands of years apart, it seems obvious that the artists were not interested in depicting a realistic *scene*, or a fresco, for that matter, no matter how perfectly executed each animal is.

The absence of any narrative is reinforced by another common feature of all the paintings. Even though the Paleolithic artists were careful to depict the animals in very energetic postures (many appear to be running at full speed), they never gave them the least bit of hard ground to stand on, by drawing even a single line under their hooves, although they didn't hesitate to capitalize on any naturally occurring cracks in the wall's surface to create a similar effect. It takes no particular skill to draw such a line; on the contrary, it would seem to be an almost instinctual gesture, since this is something that even small children will do naturally. But the prehistoric artists did not give it a second thought. As a result, their animals float on the surface of the wall, out of space and time, an effect that certainly added to the impression the paintings made on the people who discovered them. Looking a little like the airborne violinists and lovers that Chagall painted, these hefty herbivores appear to be flying, as if gravity and their environment had no pull over them whatsoever. As tempting as it is to draw romantic interpretations from this observation, it is only a statement of fact: the ground is never drawn under the animals' hooves.

No ground, but also nothing one might expect to see in the presence of animals: not a single flower or blade of grass, or plants or trees at all. No rocks either, or rivers or streams, or hills or mountains, and no sun or moon. Nor is there any hut, or village, or encampment. There is no landscape or setting at all, and there is no point in looking for them: they are not anywhere in the caves. In only the rarest and least significant cases is there any evidence of human life in the paintings. The much speculated upon and frequently photographed Panel of the Wounded Man at Lascaux (a particularly mysterious exception, hence its notoriety), has no other paintings near it, and its very awkward, almost childlike style, is in no way representative of the mastery of the animal images. We did not give this example any further thought. On the other hand, all the other paintings consist of animals and only animals; in more than two hundred sites, the natural surroundings of these beasts is never evoked. Sometimes superimposed, often in close proximity, with no apparent order or evident method or even any concern for scale, the paintings therefore appear as so many perfect, yet separate images.

Besides the question of the paintings themselves, another element to be considered is their physical environment which, in and of itself, provides a grandiose and fascinating decor, even when only experienced through high-definition photographs. The long caves found in France's Périgord, Ardèche, and Morvan regions are not painted yet they are famously spellbinding, evoking, paradoxically, both fear and a sense of calm in visitors who brave the year-round cool temperatures to experience their power for themselves. How much more impressive it would be to experience the caves by oil lamp or torchlight, which would illuminate dramatically the concretions and tormented rock faces.

On the other hand, it's evident that these sites do not lend themselves to art, even the prehistoric kind: the walls curve and twist and present recesses and ledges that would force the artist into the most contorted positions imaginable. Moreover, it would have been almost impossible to stand back from the paintings to view them as a whole. At Altamira, the bisons in the Great Hall would have hung very low over the artist's head as he worked and he would never have been able to gaze upon the whole scene at one time.

Paleolithic artists certainly didn't choose the easiest conditions in which to work, yet they made the most of them: neither bumps nor hollows, holes nor inclines, dampened their ardor nor reined in their creativity. No matter the obstacle, they painted, and did so always with the same confidence, executing huge figures at times. The case is certainly unique in the history of humanity; certainly, no other artists have been able to paint in the dark, as they did (there are very few examples of blind artists). Perhaps it was not necessary for them to see at all. A contemporary artist could hardly do as well, confronted with the same imposing challenges, whereas the prehistoric painters seem not to have been bothered in the least, completing every figure they began, with only some exceptions. Yet even in those cases, they finished the outline and did so with as much skill as they painted their best work.

Picasso declared famously of the cave paintings, "There is not one among us who can paint like that," and it is true that no art school of his day was teaching how to draw on an inclined surface already covered with other drawings. Clearly, either these were extraordinary artists, or there is another explanation that escapes us. More precisely, there remains another mystery to be solved in these immense caverns: not only do the prehistoric artists seem nonplussed by the naturally occurring hurdles to their work, they may even have sought out these difficulties. In all these caves, which consist of series of interconnected and more or less accessible rooms, galleries, and tunnels, the vast majority of the paintings are found in the darkest regions of the caves, and often in the sections that lie the furthest underground. For some, as yet inexplicable reason, the prehistoric painters showed no interest in working in the brighter, more accessible chambers of the caves or on large, unobstructed walls that would have posed no challenges to their painting. For example, there are places where the artists preferred narrow tunnels to smoother walls nearby, even when this meant having to continue the painting on a low, rough ceiling.

What explanation can there be for their choosing these areas and making their task so much more difficult? In all the history of art, at least as we conceive of it, a work is made to be seen. Usually, an artist deliberately seeks out favorable conditions for creating a piece of art as well as for viewing it. But the artists of the Upper Paleolithic Period did not think as we do. Long after the caves were discovered, we still find paintings that look as if they were deliberately hidden from view. Why devote considerable time and energy to a work of art that hardly anyone will ever see? There must be more to their motives than meets the eye, something we do not understand from our very different perspective on artistic intention.

What does an artist need to draw? A tool, first of all; any piece of charcoal will do. More importantly, however, one needs room to draw. Every parent knows that, beginning around the age of four, a child will fill any clean surface or paper he finds with his drawings. Not so for prehistoric man, absurd as it seems, and there lies a mystery. He was apparently not driven by this same urge, and painting over existing drawings did not frustrate him in the least. Any artist working today would rub out as best he could whatever images were already on the surface to clear some space and allow a clean perspective on his work. Prehistoric man? Never. He disregards his fellow artists' creations, painting right over them with the same ease as if nothing were there, allowing his new outlines to get scrambled in the earlier ones and creating quite a tangle of shapes and forms. He probably expected that visitors to the same caves, some ten, hundred, or thousand years later, would abide by the same logic and leave new images on top of his, with the same charcoal outlines and the same yellow or red chalk.

These innumerable superimpositions beg the question of their meaning. In the Apse section of Lascaux, hundreds of paintings of various sizes (ranging from a few meters to a few centimeters) are so intertwined that they are barely distinguishable. One specialist observed that the author of these images "must have encountered difficulties in the course of his work." In some caves, the images are so thickly layered (probably the work of many different artists), that they can only be "seen" by tracing painstakingly over each of them, as Abbé Breuil did. A chronological dating of the bulls in Lascaux's Great Hall has proven that the images were added over a very long time, spanning six distinct periods.[6]

How can we explain this illogical practice of painting over and over again in the same place? Is it possible that the artists were working in the dark? Why create something no one can see? The word *palimpseste* is often evoked in light of this phenomenon, a term which refers to the calligraphed manuscripts produced during the Middle Ages on costly materials (usually on vellum, made from the skin of a still-born calf) which, owing to their value, were reused rather than discarded. But the monks charged with the task of copying texts carefully cleaned all traces of earlier writing from the calfskin, so that no comparison is really possible between the monks' efforts to ensure a clean slate and the tangled images of the caves.

There is no such "palimpseste" in these caves; very rarely do we find evidence that the the artists attempted to efface the pre-existing drawings and they chose again and again to paint on the same walls. Their mastery in such conditions seems highly impressive to us today. It

---

[6] Norbert Anjoulat, *Lascaux, le geste, l'espace et le temps*, Seuil, 2004, p. 66.

is nearly impossible to draw well over a clear, existing image, and we cannot fathom why they should have wanted to do so. Since the Paleolithic artists ignored entire, clean walls and chose rather to cluster their drawings on the same spaces, just next to those unused walls, it would seem that certain areas of the caves were deemed more suitable than others for their intentions, so much so that they would come back to them over and over again, even at the risk of diminishing the clarity of the images. Could it be that this was a deliberate choice?

IX

What conclusions can we draw from this particular phenomenon and whatever it might imply? As a general rule, ever since people have created art, they have been driven by respect and even passion for their chosen craft. In turn, their skill and talent have granted them a particular place among their contemporaries, who view them as people invested with a special knowledge, much like doctors, or virtuoso musicians or men of the cloth. Having acquired a level of discernment and proficiency through lengthy training, they merit particular consideration. But this position does not come without risks, and these "Artists" have fiercely guarded the secrets of their profession, speaking of it only with similarly impassioned individuals. One thing they share is surely the respect they feel for their peers and for their predecessors, as they can certainly appreciate the hard work that these others have invested in mastering their art. Michelangelo, for example, refused to paint over

Botticelli's frescos in the Sistine Chapel, as outdated as they were thought to be and despite the insistence of his patrons. He must have feared dishonoring himself by destroying these vestiges of the Early Renaissance. Is there a musician in the world who would dare correct Mozart?

The hundreds of superimposed paintings in the caves certainly prove that prehistoric artists were not as scrupulous. What is more surprising, however, is that they never erased the earlier drawings; these they ignored, preferring instead to paint directly over them. It's as if they didn't see what they were doing..

Strange, indeed. But is there something else going on here? Perhaps the artists treated the existing drawings so carelessly because they felt these were of no particular value or exhibited no special talent. Knowing full well the significance of the paintings and how they were made, they regarded the drawings as no more than what these represented to them: outdated information, of no practical use. And so, uninspired by their ancestors' skill, they showed no consideration for what these earlier artists had left behind: they painted over everything there, then they went on their way.

X

Another fascinating characteristic of the paintings is the apparent confidence of their strokes. Despite all the obstacles we have already discussed—the uneven surfaces of the walls, their difficult access, their size, as well as the presence of the earlier paintings and the absence of any distance from what they were doing—their lines are bold and show no trace of hesitation or unevenness or correction, no matter where or when they were made. This is even true for those rare, unfinished drawings. From the back of a wooly mammoth to the profile of a bear, there is never any hint of error. The authors of the paintings could even take risks, choosing to paint a horse without drawing its outline, using pigment only to fill the space it was meant to occupy on the wall.

The evocative power of these works is startling, and their beauty is undeniable. Similarly, but even more impressively, the artists used color to shade in a zone outlined only by handprints to create an elephant. From a distance, there is a perfectly visible pachyderm on the wall.

The more we look at parietal art, the more oddities we find. For example, certain animals look surprisingly alike; give or take a few details, they are almost identical. The angle varies, but not significantly, and sometimes one has the impression that the artists were attempting a radical experiment with perspective. There are also astonishing cases of anamorphosis, or the elongation of a drawing on the wall, done in such a way that the animal does not appear deformed in the least, when observed from a particular location in the cave (figure 2). Abbé Breuil referred to this phenomenon as "twisted perspective."

But the most stunning effect of all is the "Upside-Down Horse" at Lascaux. Unlike the rest of his fellow equines, who appear to be galloping toward the far end of the cave, he seems to be racing toward the ceiling on a completely vertical course. He is just as finely drawn and as perfectly proportioned as any other horse at Lascaux; only his position is unusual. One truly appreciates the striking virtuosity of these artists with this single image, which, besides being unique, measures nearly two meters.

It would take years of training to create images like these from memory, freehand and on the first try. Everyone who has studied the paintings has admired their mastery, all the more so given that "there was no room for error because no mistake could be erased without damaging the wall on which it was made."[7]

We may imagine our prehistoric ancestors as coarse and vulgar, but they were extremely talented artists. Fortunately for our modern day egos, they were not perfect at everything, and it's worth considering next the weaknesses or failings of their paintings.

---

[7] Yannik Le Guillou, "La Galerie des Croisillons," *La Grotte Chauvet. L'art des origines.* Seuil, 2010, p. 104.

XI

The faults we can find in such admirably executed works are minor but, insignificant though they are, they may shed light on some of the mysteries of parietal art. Take for example the "Cow with Collar," at Lascaux (figure 3). The image is exquisite: its body is in red ochre while its head is black and the slightest detail of its bone structure is evident in its outline, even the bulge of the pelvis just above the tail. The head looks slightly too small for the cow's body, but many animals at Lascaux are similarly proportioned, and this small example of artistic license in these otherwise realistic drawings only accentuates its elegance. It seems fair to consider that this is a stylistic effect rather than mere clumsiness. Nevertheless, just a few centimeters above its back, there is a second line, as finely executed as the first, but this one is slightly off-center. What could it mean? It seems the artist tried his hand two times here: he first drew the back of the cow, then, unsatisfied with the excellent result, repeated the line a few centimeters below the first. Such a tiny detail does not at all diminish the image's power, but is proof at least that the artists were not infallible. They drew confidently, but sometimes they felt the need to improve upon what they had already done. Reproductions of the cave paintings in art books give ample evidence that these kinds of mistakes—animals with two backs or with double outlines—are hardly rare (figure 4).

If the redrawn back of the Lascaux cow is not an isolated incident, another defect is common to almost all of the paintings: most but not all the animals are depicted without eyes. The rare times when the artists chose to include them, the eyes seem much less confidently drawn than the rest of the image. Notwithstanding the deference we owe to such venerable works of art, we have to admit the eyes look clumsily placed on certain lions whose muzzles are morphologically accurate, which would indicate that the artists knew how to draw the cranial structure of the large felines (figure 5). Were the artists aware of their particular inadequacy in this respect? We have no way of knowing whether the mistake was deliberate or inadvertent. More than half the animals are sightless, although eyes would enhance the images' overall effect.

Every artist is aware of his strengths and weaknesses, and knows, too, that he will always struggle to turn those weaknesses into strengths. Could it be that the prehistoric artists could not resolve the problem of how to depict eyes, even though they could draw the animals' morphologies almost perfectly? It seems unlikely.

Let's consider another clue, then: the eyes are not the only body part that seems to have stymied these immensely talented artists. While the cave painters were indisputably skilled at drawing the outline of an animal's musculature, they almost never added any kind of detail to the surface of the animal's body that would indicate what aspect the muscles would have as they moved under the skin, or that would show the artists' understanding of this. Those occasions when they do trace the juttting of a shoulder blade or the slope of a hindquarter, the line never extends into the silhouette; in fact, they seem incapable of accurately endowing their animals with any muscles at all. They are satisfied with the mere outline. Even when they rub color onto the bodies of their horses or their bison, it's as if the artists are feeling their way as they attempt to evoke a vaguely rounded form, so that the bellies and thighs of those horses and those bison are mere approximations of their real-life models and are even poorly drawn, at that. The outlines are so realistic and assured that we usually fail to notice any shortcomings, yet the more we look, the more we notice that the animals lack depth, as if their internal organs were missing. It begs the question of how such otherwise skilled painters could have failed to understand that it is possible to add a third dimension to an image, simply by extending the outline into the internal space of the the shape being drawn. This is very easy to do compared to memorizing the shape of a horse's nose or a lion's muzzle or a bull's neck. Yet, for twenty-five thousand years, very few of the cave painters dared to try this. Some may argue that the cows and equines at Lascaux and at many other caves are wonderfully colored inside their outlines, but this requires skillful shading or painting only, not drawing. What's more, even though the dyes used by the cave painters impart a strong visual aesthetic, they are flatly applied, with no apparent thought given to the shape of the animal being drawn. Should we conclude that the interior space of the shapes didn't interest them or that they had great difficulty imagining what to do with that space? This is a fair question; many cave drawings display the same kind of errors: sometimes the ears look askew, while, at other times, it might be an eye that is facing the viewer while the rest of the head appears in profile, or another set of eyes that sits too close to a rhino's nostrils to appear lifelike. Are these artistic liberties, stylistic experiments, or sheer clumsiness?

There are more, equally mysterious anomalies. For example, there are some very precisely proportioned and anatomically correct specimen whose hooves or tails look, when they are not simply sketched in with a few approximate lines, as if they were strangely attached to their legs or their rumps and appear out of place with the rest of their bodies (figure 6).

Far from us to judge parietal art severely or unfairly; how could we begin to pass judgement on something made so many millennia ago? Enumerating the different defects is helpful, however, to gain new understanding. After all, these minor imperfections, these particularities or limits of what the artists were capable, since they are found so frequently in drawings far removed from each other in time and geography, may just be the clues we have been seeking.

What, then, do we know so far? We know that the prehistoric artists could trace the outline of an animal with great skill, even when they purposely elongated or shrunk the size, and that they could indicate with extreme precision on that same outline the location of muscles and bones. We know also they did not draw from a living model when they painted in the caves. Does that mean that they knew how to draw from memory at the same time that they were capable of modifying an animal's true shape, with a small head or a wide abdomen or short paws, for example? Details such as these are all the more astonishing because, in all other regards, the forms perfectly resemble a head, an abdomen, etc. However, as perfectly drawn as the outlines are, any realistic details there may be on the inside of the outlines appear to be added haphazardly, one would almost say crudely.[8] Apparently, prehistoric man was a master at outlines but not particularly talented at adding true-to-life details to the interior zone of the drawing. On the one hand, extraordinary ability; on the other, evident clumsiness. This "willful disinterest for internal detail"[9] is indeed difficult to explain, but nonetheless true.

Let us also not forget the most common characteristic of the paintings, found in all the caves, practically without exception: the animals are always depicted in profile. It's as if it never occurred to a single artist to draw them head on, although this is easier to do; it is much harder, for example, to draw two symmetrical bull's horns than to wrestle with the question of perspective if the horns are to be shown in profile. Perhaps, like the Egyptians, who followed a definite rule wherein the body is shown from one side while the head is turned to face the viewer, the Paleolithic artists could not approach their subjects from any other angle. This same phenomenon is found in the Babylonian frescoes and Ishtar's Gate, whose lions are also shown in profile. Be that as it may, the rule followed by the prehistoric cave artists is surprising because of the length of time

---

[8] The remark applies to drawings only, not paintings.

[9] Emmanuel Guy, "La Grotte Chauvet : un art totalement homogène?" Paléoesthétique.com, Feb. 2004.

(thirty thousand years) and the geographical area (thousands of kilometers) involved.

A last observation: once it has been established that the fluidity of the outlines does not extend to the interior spaces of the forms, it is possible to disassociate the two. The reason that so many animals resemble each other is that—even though they have been colored differently and the angles vary slightly—they are always shown in the same profile. In all the painted caves, there exist series of very similar drawings. At Chauvet, for example, there are magnificent profiles of horses whose heads closely resemble each other, although the way in which they were shaded may differ. Chauvet also contains a series of nearly intertwined lions' heads. Here again, we see the same profile repeated in close proximity; only the coloring and the interior details are different (figure 7). Although each lion seems to have its own personality, we understand the group to form a single pride. There is also a series of five deer heads in a line, which has been interpreted as a herd crossing a river in single file (figure 8). Their antlers are nearly identical, with the same form and number of branches: a similarity that never occurs in nature. There can be no doubt that the same head was drawn five times. The logical conclusion is that the artist of this supposed herd didn't draw the heads freehand but, as strange as it sounds, either traced or stenciled them.

XII

Tracing? Stenciling? Could the prehistoric cave painters have been familiar with such a "modern" technique? The idea seems preposterous, but there are plenty of absurdities in this tale of generations of artists who would have found time to develop their skills between bison hunting trips, and their drawings of animals, repeated over and over again and piled on top of each other in an almost indistinguishable mass, exhibiting the same level of mastery—as well as the same defects— over thousands of years, and which were apparently not meant to be seen, but were painted in the furthest recesses of caves instead of in much more easily accessible areas. There seems to be no possible explanation for proceeding in such an illogical and incomprehensible manner, except that they were indeed tracing their animal figures. But how?

Children know how hard it is to draw their favorite comic book character. Luckily, there is tracing paper: a single sheet placed over the dashing image of the comic strip hero is all it takes to reproduce a similarly captivating silhouette. Nothing could be easier than to run a pencil along his figure on the opposite side of the same tracing film, then place that drawing on a clean sheet of paper. Voilà; the hero appears again, although he may seem to float in space, a little crookedly perhaps too. It may only be an outline, but it is an outline nonetheless, and quite well drawn.

Obviously, back when wooly mammoths still walked the earth, this was not how it was done. But let's consider the whole picture, so to speak: what would be the point of reproducing the same images for twenty-five thousand years if these were time-consuming to make and had no actual purpose? The cave paintings were useful in some way, served some essential function, were perhaps considered vital to the community even, but creating them could not have been particularly difficult or the artists working over all these millennia would have simplified the procedure or developed a method that would have saved time and energy, such as happened for stone-cutting. If not, the drawings would have become progressively more schematic, to finish as abstract signs, just like the ideogrammatic alphabets of the Middle East and Asia. But not here, not even over such an immense period of time: the painting technique underwent no significant changes. This must mean that it was not overly difficult and that excellent results were easily obtained. The solution must therefore lie in some kind of mechanical solution, a simple "trick," that only needed to be learned once. Why do we still shape arrows and build fires and weave ropes much the same way our ancestors did? Because these methods work, and always do. So also, the reason that little changed over the fifteen thousand years that separate Chauvet and Lascaux must be that the artists had an easy, fail-proof technique and there was no need to tamper with it.

Without a doubt, all these drawings present too many similarities to not be the product of the same method, one which would not rely purely on artistic talent. That is not to say that the artists were not skilled, but they did as any intelligent person would: they developed a tool that minimized difficulties and saved time. Prehistoric man invented the spear-thrower, to achieve greater velocity with a javelin, and he invented the bow, as well, yet no one has ever accused him of cheating at the noble art of hunting. So when he wanted to draw in the caves, he found a way to do it, unless the means gave way to the practice, and the technique first gave him the idea of drawing.

What was this mysterious method? To begin with, it probably did not require much instruction to master but could have been quickly understood and easily passed on to succeeding generations of artists. It would have allowed anyone to draw the outline of an animal, faultlessly, anywhere he wished in the caves, even in the darkest corner and on the most irregular surface. He would have been able to draw his animals to any scale he wished, sometimes huge, sometimes minuscule, with or without anamorphosis, even when the wall was already covered by drawings. Does such a technique exist and could it have been discovered so many millennia ago? The answer is yes, and the method is among the simplest and the most efficient ever known.

Figure 1. Lascaux, Hall of Bulls.

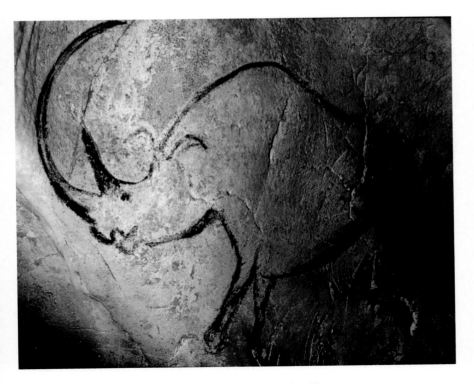

Figure 2. Anamorphic rhinoceros in the Chauvet cave.

Figure 3. Cow in Lascaux.

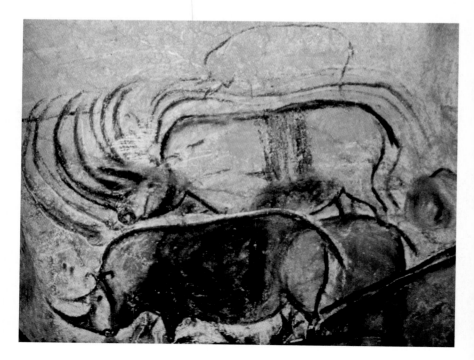

Figure 4. Two rhinos in the Chauvet cave.

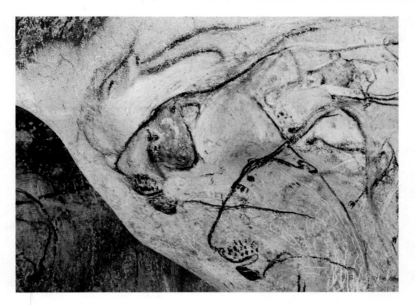

Figure 5. Lions in the Chavuet cave.

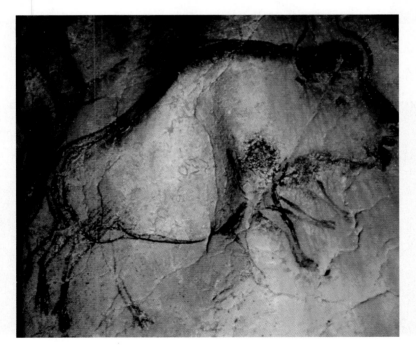

Figure 6. Bison in the Chauvet cave.

Figure 7. Lions in the Chavuet cave.

Figure 8. A frieze of deer in Lascaux.

XIII

I'm descending the staircase. I've just wished my eight-year-old son goodnight, turned off the light, and shut the door. I can't let go of the idea I had a moment ago. So I turn back up the stairs, hesitate on the landing, then reopen the door and turn on the light. I begin to distinguish the form of my half-asleep child. I look again at the shadow that his bedside lamp is throwing on the ceiling: a plastic dinosaur he had placed near the light on his nightstand appears twice as big on the opposite wall, stretching all the way to the ceiling. I see other small figurines lying on the floor: a disarticulated robot, a stuffed kangaroo, and some plastic horses are strewn about on an improbable farm where cows, tigers, and dinosaurs all live together. I pick up the horses and place them in front of the small lamp. Their shadows loom large on the wall. Their impeccably modeled forms create equally perfect shadows. A prehistoric fresco suddenly appears before me on the white wall of my child's bedroom, just as real as any sophisticated recreation of the caves.

XIV

A plastic elephant no more than twelve centimeters long from tail to trunk, straight from a Chinese factory, served as my first guinea pig. For equipment, I found a fat candle that had been lying around in the kitchen, while a well-used, well-grooved, nearly torn-in-half piece of packing cardboard was tacked up onto the wall of my studio. A stick of charcoal was enlisted to do what it does best, since the charcoal used today is nothing more than a piece of burned willow, more commonly known as wood charcoal.

My son was proud to show me how easily he could execute the drawing I asked of him. By the light of the single candle, whose glow bathed the room in the luminescence of a Georges De Latour painting, even a child can carefully trace the silhouette of a perfectly proportioned elephant in profile. He only has to follow the line that separates light from shadow, without second-guessing himself. His hand is steady as he easily moves his charcoal along the line where shadow fades into light. Standing on a shoe box placed close to the lamp, the little elephant makes an excellent model, never stirring once.

I turn the overhead light back on. The candle light pales suddenly and the shadow on the old, bent piece of cardboard disappears just as quickly, but the outline of the elephant now floats in its place. I mention to my budding artist that an eye is missing and that he should draw one in. "Just like that?" "Just like that." He does, then adds, "Drawing like this is kind of like cheating. It's too easy."

In any case, the first experiment is encouraging and the process works like a charm: by projecting the shadow of any form—an animal figurine, for example—onto a wall, absolutely anyone can easily trace around this sort of Chinese shadow puppet and end up with an outline that perfectly matches the shape of the model used. Details and colors can be added later to the resulting drawing.

XV

Over the following months, as I carefully sifted through the research I had gathered on the painted caves, my interest in the stories they could hold began to wane. Something else seemed far more important. What was this idea of mine? A discovery? An illusion? A coincidence? If my gut feeling could be trusted, I had to explore the question further, and I had to start by finding out if someone else had had the same idea as I did in my son's bedroom and if my theory had already been examined and rejected. I would first need to read all the existing literature on the caves, from the oldest studies to the most difficult. The next and all important step would be to perform a few more experiments while trying to replicate as faithfully as possible the conditions in which the cave paintings were made so many millennia ago. But as luck would have it, I was living in Brittany, where there are hardly any caves at all. What did it matter, though? Who would let me in their cave anyway, to try my own hand at prehistoric painting? I had to find another way. Finally, though less importantly, if my theory proved true, I would still need to answer this one simple but troubling question: why did no one ever think of this before?

One thing was certain: I had to prove by any means possible that my explanation could be supported by what was already known for certain about the caves. As intriguing and new as my idea seemed to me, for it to be true, prehistoric man would have had to have figurines like the ones I used for my first experiment, although not made of Chinese plastic of course. The theory itself was not implausible, but it needed to be supported with concrete facts.

We know from the kinds of objects made by most early peoples that well before they began to draw (a hardly instinctive process of abstraction, as we have seen), they sculpted and modeled. Whatever their chosen material and its durability, from clay to wood or stone, the desire to recreate reality in a three-dimensional form has always existed. Judging from the wealth of artifacts uncovered by archeological digs—charms, amulets, fetishes, toys, fashioned from both ordinary and precious materials and fulfilling many functions—mankind has always carved as an expression of his world. Among all the figures produced, animals are a particularly popular subject.

Modeling or sculpting a form no matter how realistic is never as difficult as drawing. With the point of a brush or a pencil, an illustrator draws a single line to represent the dimensions he sees or remembers. Modeling, on the other hand, offers the artist many more possibilities. If he is working with a soft material like clay, he can proceed as cautiously as he wishes, enlarging and reducing as necessary, and he can monitor his progress as he goes, observing his work from any angle, trying anything out, and coming gradually closer to the shape he holds in his eye or in his mind. A material like wood or stone does not offer the same possibilities since any cuts the artist makes cannot be replaced, but he can try out his ideas in the form of a smaller model. He can also sand and polish his work in such a way as to emphasize its curves, and, if he has his model before him, he can constantly compare his work with it. Although as much talent is needed of a great sculptor as of a great painter, and while the skills needed in each case differ, it is certainly easier to arrive at a passably good result by modeling. For example, shaping a perfect circle is easier and more rapidly done than drawing one freehand.

If it was not impossible that the cave painters used sculpted figurines to cast shadows on the walls, the existence of these statuettes remained to be proven. This promised to be difficult because, even if they did exist, they might have been too fragile to survive to the present day. It had to be hoped that the Paleolithic sculptors used durable materials and that their statues would be hard to break, or had been invested with an important symbolic power, so that generations of artists would have passed them on over millennia. Only one sculptor would be needed initially to make a single figurine that succeeding generations could use and reuse to trace their drawings in the caves.

The first large encyclopedia of prehistory that I found in a used bookstore confirmed for me that such objects did indeed exist. Dozens had been discovered, in fact, in the same geographical locations as the caves, and the majority of the subjects were animal figures. Dating had found them to be as old as the paintings, with which they also share many stylistic similarities, but, strangely, no one had ever developed a theory concerning their function. In other words, these animal figurines were sturdy enough to have lasted until now and they were sufficiently elaborate and realistic to cast a perfect shadow of a horse or a bull on the wall.

Among the various pieces of sculpture dated to the successive Paleolithic toolmaking cultures, there are a few naturalistic figures dating from the Aurignacian period, more than one hundred from the Gravettian,[10] and a few dozen from the Magdalenian.[11] Some of these are in wood, such as the "whinnying horse" head at Mas d'Azil

---

[10] In other words, 28,000 to 22,000 years ago.

[11] Marcel Otte, *La Préhistoire*, De Boeck, 2009, p. 187. The Magdalenian period dates from 18,000 to 12,000 years ago.

in France's Ariège region, while others were made from the bones or ivory of mammoths, such as were found in caves in the Swabian Jura mountains of southwest Germany. These animals appear as if identical to those found at Chauvet and in many other caves—felines, mammoths, bears, rhinoceros, horses, bison—and some are at least as old as the Chauvet paintings.[12] Clay figurines were extremely fragile, of course, and very few have been found.[13] Only two bison in the Tuc d'Audoubert cave have survived in good condition.[14]

A few of these figurines are in museum collections. One example is a magnificent horse discovered in the Espélugues cave, in Lourdes, France, and housed at the

---

[12] Michel Lorblanchet noted the resemblance of the animals found at Chauvet and in the Swabian Jura, remarking that "some similarities can be detected in the head profiles of the felines" (*La Naisssance de l'art. Genèse de l'art phréhistorique*, Editions Errance, 1999, p. 261).

[13] A painting by the Czech artist Zdenek Burian (1905–1981), in the collection of the Moravské Muzeum at the Institute Anthropos in Brno, shows a prehistoric man fashioning animal statues in clay.

[14] The bisons' two right feet are clearly shaped, with detailed hooves, while the back left foot is absent and the front left foot is faintly sketched. This manner of drawing the feet—clearly shaped on one side, barely suggested on the other—occurs frequently in parietal art.

Ivory horse,
Espelugues caves, Lourdes
(National Archaeological Musuem,
Saint-Germain-en-Laye, France)

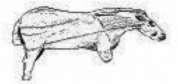

Horse's head, neighing
reindeer antlers, Mas d'Azil
(National Archaeological Musuem,
Saint-Germain-en-Laye, France)

Animal figurines from the Paleolithic Period.

National Archeological Museum of Saint-Germain-en-Laye. Most are small, in general, measuring a dozen centimeters or so, sometimes less. The majority of these have been broken or only a fragment remains but the fact that any of these have survived to the present seems like a small miracle and is proof than many more once existed, in different sizes, and were indeed produced in great number in the Upper Paleolithic Period.

XVI

Everything seemed to be coming together; with the existence of the statues now firmly established, my idea didn't seem so crazy anymore. If it could hold weight as a rational hypothesis, it was time to test it.

Of course, I had no way of getting my hands on a prehistoric statue. I would have to use my imagination and do the best with whatever I could find. A hunting trip to a toy store was all I needed to assemble a small game park. Some of these plastic and rubber figurines demonstrated an admirable likeness, while others were simpler, less detailed. In order to have the largest variety of sizes at my disposal, I even located some flat, plywood cut-outs of horses.

With a wide selection of figurines at my disposal, the next all-important question was lighting. It probably doesn't occur to anyone studying the paintings in the pages of a photo album that those marvelous images would not be possible without electricity. However, what the Paleolithic artists could see of their own work and of the surrounding caves is vastly different than what we can see with the help of modern lighting. In fact, the drawings can really only be appreciated in the belly of the caves themselves, in places that are very difficult to illuminate and that can only be reached after a long journey through sinuously winding corridors. It's here that prehistoric man created them, in galleries so plunged in darkness that it is almost impossible to see more than a single painting at a time.

A torch gives off a vacillating light, whose incessant waverings cannot be replicated by electric lighting. If I was going to recreate anything like the actual conditions in which the paintings were made, it was out of the question to use a modern light source. Mammoth oil being in short supply these days, I knew I would have to find an oil lamp of some kind. Several had been discovered in the caves, even at Lascaux, which had turned up one of the most famous and beautiful specimens: an oil burner in pink sandstone.

I won't go into great detail about my quest to find a proper oil lamp and the right kind of fuel for it. What I will say is that, while oil lamps are still sold, can often be pretty, and are even rather expensive at times, they don't give off much light. After several disappointing attempts, a family heirloom was pressed into service: a very old clay lamp that fairly resembled the kind of burners used in Antiquity, and that my parents had received as a gift from a friend who had brought it back from a North African desert. Its exact age was unknown, but it was evidently very old and it had been left to me after my parents' death. I removed it from its display case and carefully filled it with oil, rolling a tuft of cotton from the bathroom into a wick. Although it hadn't been used for centuries, the old lamp glowed again. No genie appeared but the darkened room was soon bathed in a faint yet magnificent light that lent everything in the room an impressive air of reddish mystery. It was lovely.

One advantage of this kind of ancient lamp is that it's possible to regulate the amount of light it gives off by lengthening or shortening the wick, a trick known perhaps to prehistoric man as well. One disadvantage is that it gives off a dense smoke that doesn't obscure the light but that can be thick, as it became apparent as soon as I turned the electricity back on.

The last hurdle was to find a place to perform my experiment. For my "cave," I finally decided on a very old cellar, with roughly cemented walls stained by saltpeter and damp. This seemed to me a fair replacement for the prehistoric galleries. In order to suspend the figurines so the light could shine past them, I used a soldering iron to make a hole in the abdomen of the each animal and then screwed these onto pieces of wood I had cut to various heights.

With these three questions answered, the experiments could begin. I began by filling in all the possible cracks in the walls that might let the outside light in. Next, using a naked lightbulb to see by, I placed the oil lamp slightly above the ground. Its flame danced around and a dark plume of smoke rose. In front of it, perched on a stick that I had attached to a mostly stable support, I placed a plastic figurine of a galloping horse measuring a dozen or so centimeters long. I flipped off the light switch and waited a few moments for my eyes to adjust to the darkness. The lamp seemed weak so I pulled the wick further out of the oil, which increased the light's intensity. The shadow appeared on the wall, a bit blurry but perfectly visible. I moved the lamp slightly. The shadow fluttered, faded completely for a moment then returned suddenly, larger and more imposingly. It flickered again then became immobile.

The first thing I noticed was that, while my set-up worked, it wasn't easy to control. The shadows cast by the lamp were not very big: the size and intensity of the flame directly influenced the dimensions of the image produced. My little experiment in the storage cellar could hardly create anything comparable to the huge drawings of the caves, but it was easy enough to produce a clear projection of an animal silhouette on the cellar wall. It was also very moving to make the same gesture that the prehistoric artists did and trace the outline of that first drawing with a piece of charcoal.

As I did, I had to forget everything I knew about drawing. My line had to be as neutral as possible to avoid any of my own influences. I had to think as the prehistoric artists did. In reality, however, my fears were unfounded: I couldn't see anything I was doing in the half-light as I traced along the edges of the shadow. The line faded into the darkness as quickly as I drew it and there was no possible way to correct it. I tried only to trace as consistently as I could, all the while suspecting I was making mistakes every time I moved or stopped for a moment, as there was no way of knowing where I had left off. In other words, I had no choice but to draw as surely as possible, along the neck or the withers, never wavering in the slightest. I tried not to be distracted by the noise of the charcoal as it wore itself out on the rough surface of the wall or by my own breathing, which was a bit labored because of the smoke of the lamp.

It took me less than a minute to draw the outline of a figure about fifty centimeters long from a model four times smaller. Successive attempts made (and filmed) over the following days backed up my first impression: it couldn't be easier or faster to do.

I have a hard time accurately expressing my surprise when I looked at that first outline under the electric light. On the decrepit cellar wall, a horse with no eyes raced along as if floating in the air. My stops and starts were visible but the overall result bore an undeniable resemblance to the cave paintings. The uneven surface of the wall contrasted with the ease with which the drawing seemed to have been made, despite the cracks and bumps. In fact, these irregularities had unexpectedly added details that heightened the drawing's power. Even though I had drawn for years, I could never have traced a similarly fluid outline freehand. All my training as an illustrator was for nothing: the method worked like a charm, and even better than I had imagined.

XVII

Rather unnerved by the rapidity of the entire process and the sharpness of that first outline, I traced all afternoon. Each new silhouette was a source of new revelations—some accidentally so—but all of them shed light, beyond a shadow of a doubt so to speak, on some of the questions I had been asking myself about parietal art.

For starters, I learned that the darkness had to be absolute. Even the slightest ray of light coming under the door or through the lock made the shadow less apparent. Whether this was an optical illusion or an actual physical phenomenon or whether the human eye cannot adapt completely to the dark when a light source is present, I couldn't say, but I soon realized that if the light hitting the figurine is at all weak, there must be complete darkness in order to draw.

This would explain why the rooms of the caves that are closest to the entrances were never chosen by the prehistoric artists as a canvas for their paintings, even when those rooms offered smoother walls and were easily accessible. Finally, the use of the darkest rooms of the caves now made sense, and I understood why the artists ignored those walls that I had thought would have been the best for painting. Absolutely no outside light could filter in if the outline was to appear as clearly as possible and if the artists were to draw the greatest number of figures possible. This has to explain why the first gallery at Altamira, where the daylight reaches, contains no paintings, while the succeeding rooms and tunnels are overflowing with art. At Niaux also, not a single drawing is to be found near the entrance, and at Chauvet, though its first room lies in darkness, only its back wall, which stands more than eighty meters from the entrance, contains drawings. This offers an explanation also for the dissimilarities between the realism of the animal motifs in the caves and the petroglyphs found in the deserts of Africa. Those engravings, which were made in daylight, are highly stylized, unlike the cave paintings. Clearly, the sites of the drawings were not chosen for any ritualistic motives or because the artists lived there; very simply, rather, these sites best suited the artists' purposes.

That isn't to say that the procedure is entirely straightforward, even when all the conditions are met. As effortless as my first experiment was, the harder some of my later attempts were, and inexplicably so. Part of the difficulty lies with the distances separating the lamp, the figurine, and the wall, which must be carefully adjusted. Yet no matter how many times I tried, I never managed to arrive at a helpful rule of thumb that would make it possible to consistently obtain a clear shadow, or even a discernible one for that matter. It seemed at times that no matter how I moved the lamp or the figurine, the shadow never fell because I had willed it to do so but because it was then that the *shadow chose to project itself*, and I had to be patient and await that moment. As the flame would suddenly shine with greater, and unexpected intensity, owing perhaps to the rate at which the wick was being consumed or the quality of the oil, a precise shadow of the animal would be thrown on the wall when I least expected it and would stand immobile there despite the fluctuations of the flame. I was forced to draw the silhouette wherever the shadow *chose* to put itself. It was frustrating and discouraging at best, impossible in fact, to try to place the shadow myself: nothing I did, no adjusting of the lamp helped. I could wear myself out moving it around, turning it a bit one way or the other, or I might place the figure closer to the lamp or to the wall, but there was no predicting when the shadow would appear, inexplicably but clearly. Sometimes the shadow would wrap itself halfway up the ceiling, but I never understood why or how. Those were the moments when I was simply happy to be able to trace it, relieved that it had allowed me to immortalize it with a line of charcoal on the wall.

It seems folly to believe that the prehistoric artists could determine with any precision the best places to leave their drawings; the moods of the flame and the caprices of the shadow made those decisions for them, and it was not usually the smoothest or the most open wall that could best accommodate the figurines' shadows. The slightest breath or draft of air could cause the flame to flicker sufficiently to prevent a shadow from being cast. Again, this explains why there are no drawings in the rooms exposed to drafts; a clearly defined shadow requires an immobile flame.

Chance plays a significant role in this method and there are doubtless many factors that contribute to it. We could regulate the process by substituting a flashlight for an oil lamp, and there would be good reasons for doing this. For myself, hardly better equipped as I was than the prehistoric artists, I never could understand why a shadow appeared distinctly or not at all, even though I tried again and again. This unpredictability is probably one explanation for the seemingly bizarre positionings of many paintings.

However, when I did succeed and I managed to replicate the success of my first drawing, I arrived at another conclusion: a three-dimensional figurine does not create the most traceable shadow. A bas-relief or a cut-out works far better. The curves of a fully fleshed, three-dimensional statue blur on the wall, but those of a flat form do not. Moreover, among the surviving Paleolithic figurines, many are quite flat and resemble more closely a bas-relief than a fully three-dimensional statue, as if their actual depth mattered less than the silhouette they created.

Several other questions I had concerning the characteristics of the paintings were answered accidentally over the course of my experiments. Once, when I was tracing the shadow of a new animal, a slight movement on my part caused me to bump the stick holding the figurine. Although the movement was hardly noticeable, it was enough to shift the shadow and to force me to start my drawing over again. When I turned on the electric light, I saw I had drawn an animal with two backs, just like the famous "Cow with Collar" at Lascaux, or, in the same cave, the two bulls whose backs are drawn with both a thick black line and a lighter one in the same color just above the first, or "Red Cow" in the Axial Gallery, whose chest seems to have been drawn twice. The least movement of the figurine must have caused the artist to draw his outline again, and those strange features that seem so incomprehensible otherwise were the unintentional result.[15] Another mystery of parietal art was solved.

---

[15] This also affects the interpretation of the Eight-Legged Bison at Chauvet: the desired effect seems to be to represent the speed of the animal in motion rather than to visually break down the movement of its gait.

In the same way, I realized quickly that when the figurine is dislodged from its stick, it is absolutely impossible to reposition it in the same way so as to continue the outline where it was left off. If the model changes position in any way, the drawing cannot be completed, no matter how promisingly it was begun. This explains the many cave paintings that were perfectly started but remain unfinished or were hardly begun at all: a mammoth's back or a bear's muzzle, and nothing more. These formerly puzzling interruptions are puzzling no longer.[16] This also suggests why these fragments seem, at times, to bear no resemblance to the rest of the animal: tracing a shape rather than drawing it allows the artist to begin the outline wherever he wishes and to stop it just as abruptly.

Other discoveries would prove to be even more astounding. For example, in many of the cave paintings, the feet or tails are barely sketched in, but if these parts of the figurine are very fine or small, they do not project a shadow onto the wall, and so the artist must draw them in freehand. So much for the theory that stated the artists were obeying a particular style of

---

[16] For some of the drawings, the line breaks off in the area of the animal's underbelly. If the figurines were placed on a support of some kind at the level of their belly, such as I had done, the outline would logically stop at that point of contact.

drawing by omitting the feet and tails; in fact, this is just the result of the quality of the shadow cast by the figurine.

I experimented with some other ideas, as well: if the shadow is projected at an angle onto the wall, will the figurine's silhouette still appear? Yes, but the outline looks strange; unintentionally, I had created a distorted, even deformed image: in a word, an example of anamorphosis. Once again, the method employed by the prehistoric artists explains the oddities of the paintings; the shortened, elongated, and deformed animals found in the caves are not a stylistic effect but rather result from the attempt of projecting a shadow onto a wall, in the capricious and unpredictable conditions of the caves. Those examples of "twisted perspective" could not be produced freehand; another mystery solved.

I noticed something else by pure chance. Once, as I was getting ready to trace the silhouette of a new horse, the figurine, which I had failed to attach firmly to its stick, spun around, and suddenly I was looking at an upside-down horse. It was perfectly proportioned; only its orientation was wrong. It was just like the horse at Lascaux, whose strange position has given rise to many interpretations, one of which holds that the picture represents a hunting technique in which the quarry was run over a cliff. Here again, the method makes it just as easy to draw any shape upside-down as right side up, because the gesture required of the artist is the same and the process works however which way the model is oriented. Moreover, the proportions of the upside-down horse at Lascaux are identical to those of the other equines present there, and just as fluidly drawn too.

One more curiosity was explained, if any new explanation was needed by this time, when I projected the shadow of an elephant on top of the drawing of a rhinoceros that I had recently finished. The wall was already filled with images. Would it be difficult to draw the little pachyderm there, I wondered. Absolutely not: the light was so faint that I could not see the rhinoceros at all. Any number of animals could be superimposed in this way to create the "palimpseste effect" that has puzzled researchers for so long. I had the strange, maybe even ancestral, impression that the prehistoric artists were not trying their hand at superimposition but were just drawing on a wall. Wherever the shadow fell, the artists traced it, and so did I.

The sheer numbers of inextricably entwined animals, piled up and mixed up in a crowded space but never at the expense of the other drawings, has long mystified specialists. They marvel at "the abundance and the multitude taking precedence over the individual"[17] in these examples of deliberate, graphic exuberance. Superimposing a drawing over an existing picture is hardly

---

[17] Carole Fritz, Gilles Tosello, "Le Secteur des Chevaux," *La Grotte Chauvet. L'art des origines*, Seuil, 2010, p. 11.

instinctual, however; doing so presupposes a method allowing the artist to easily draw on top of earlier work. Tracing the outline of a shadow in such darkness that it makes it impossible to see the older drawings seems to be the only possible way of arriving at a point where the images are so numerous they can barely be distinguished one from another.[18]

---

[18] The technique of projecting the shadow of an animal figurine also helps explain why there are so few narrative scenes involving two or more animals: a rare occurrence giving rise to much speculation. The two rhinoceroses facing off on a wall at Chauvet have been interpreted as a stand off between two rival males or as a mating dance between a male and a female. In reality, the two beasts are no more in conflict (as the position of their horns would attest, moreover) than they are in love; in both cases, the two figures were drawn separately and the artist who drew the second rhino would not have seen the first one at all. The same explanation holds at Lascaux, in the case of the two horses thought to be getting ready to mate, for the two felines who appear to be doing the same, and for the "squaring-off deer" in the Apse, where the stag on the right side appears to be attacking the other, although, as the authors of the *Dictionnaire de Lascaux* have noted, "the right-hand deer is placed much lower than its rival" (Brigitte and Gilles Delluc, *op. cit.*, p. 69).

XVIII

Later experiments in the cellar performed with some helpers confirmed all my initial observations. The drawings I made by tracing shadows—albeit with a somewhat differently powered light source than was used by the original painters—all pointed to the same conclusion: the vast majority of the cave paintings were made using this tracing technique. It may not account for all of the drawings but it was certainly the most frequently employed method. That being the case, several particularities of the paintings can be clearly established. First of all, the systematic presentation of the animals in profile was not a choice but rather the only way to distinguish the kind of animal being drawn. If a figurine was placed to face the light source, it would be difficult to tell what kind of animal was represented by the projected shadow, which would look like nothing more than a potato and would only demonstrate a competent mastery of the shape's interior details. There are a few very rare examples of animals depicted head on, and these are not realistic at all. We can barely distinguish the stylized form of a horse or a great horned owl whose head faces us while its body is seen from behind. Both are crudely sketched and poorly executed.

The similarities of the drawings could also now be justified, as well. If there are definite stylistic differences between the paintings at Chauvet and Lascaux, this must be because different styles of figurines were used there; the technique is otherwise the same.[19] There are also obvious differences in the way each artist colored and added details to the interior space of the outlines. Some were particularly good at this and, aided by their own talent, knew how to bring the profiles of their animals to life, as did the artist who drew the lions found at Chauvet whose outlines have been magnified by light touches of white and whose eyes are, for once, anatomically correct. Certainly, many other drawings did not benefit from a skilled hand going over them to correct and embellish them, and it seems in these cases that either the outline was sufficient for the purposes of the

---

[19] The sculptors must surely have been talented; only good quality statuettes could have produced such perfect, such elegant images. The question to be asked is not why the paintings resemble each other so closely but rather why the figurines were made to look like each other.

artist or that the artist was incapable of doing more than tracing the shadow.

As for the apparent assuredness of the lines and the absence of corrections, the child's play that is tracing provides all the explanation necessary. Why hesitate when nothing is easier than obediently following the shadow's contour along the wall? Moreover, the artists would have felt a certain urgency to complete their drawings while the flame and the figurine worked their magic because, as we discovered, very little is needed to disrupt the necessary conditions for tracing: if the shadow wavers, changes shape, or disappears, even the most promising drawing will never be completed. Similarly, the unevenness of the wall's surface, which would pose a challenge to any other kind of artist, mattered little in the caves; the shadows could be projected onto any "canvas" the caves presented, and tracing them with charcoal or ochre was no more difficult for all that. Cro-Magnon man even learned to make use of the natural irregularities of the surfaces on which they drew, to give the impression of depth, by using a small depression in the wall, for example, to suggest the line of the spine of a bison and to heighten the realism of the drawings.

The variety of sizes of the paintings could also be explained easily by moving the figurine in relation to the flame, to either shrink or enlarge the size of the shadow cast. The possibilities are endless, even using the same figurine; only the distance, the direction and the intensity of the light matter and there is consequently nothing strange in seeing tiny mammoths running next to enormous deer. Concerning the deer in particular, I tried drawing the shadow of the same figurine five times, each time moving the lamp or the figurine slightly. The result easily explains the five deer heads with the same antlers depicted in single file but at slightly different angles at Lascaux. Those angles would be created by a slight rotation of the figurine on its stick. The same explanation holds true for the many series of nearly identical animals drawn in close proximity in the caves: the same figurine would have served for each series.

We discussed earlier the strange lack of respect demonstrated by the prehistoric artists for the work of their predecessors, never hesitating to draw right over existing paintings as if these were already obsolete. But how could they spare these earlier drawings if they couldn't see them because of the shadows they were projecting onto the walls? Moreover, given that the artists were only tracing the outline of a shadow of a figurine, why respect something that takes so little effort that anyone can do it?

If fact, it's not even necessary to trace the outline. Sometimes the shadow is so clear and stable that the artist can simply get away with filling the space of the shadow with one or more pigments by rubbing these on the wall with his fingertips. I tried this, coloring in the shadow just to its edges, and was rewarded with the big and beautiful silhouette of a horse. A little extra attention to the hooves, and, just like at Lascaux, I had drawn an animal without ever tracing a line. The image looked slightly blurred, but that only heightened the grace and power of this horse in full gallop. So, too, I realized how the panels in the Gallery of Hands at Chauvet were made. I projected the shadow of an elephant on the wall and discovered that by covering my palms with red ochre and applying them to the shadow, I could instantaneously create a pachyderm without any need of an outline.

XIX

To return then to the list of questions I raised in the beginning of my research, it's clear that most have now been answered, in particular those concerning the technique used by the painters. More to the point, this is the first scientific explanation that can answer all the questions at once:

How did the prehistoric artists create their drawings? By tracing shadows cast on a wall by a light shone on a figurine.

How did they learn how to do it? No particular training was necessary.

Why did they always depict the animals in profile? It would not have been possible to create a recognizable shape any other way.

Why are the drawings so frequently superimposed? The artists drew wherever the shadow fell.

How did they manage to draw over other paintings without making any mistakes? Very easily in fact, since the shadow the artist projected hid the earlier paintings from his view.

Why are there so few poorly executed drawings? Because the shadow is always perfect and the artist had only to trace it.

Why were so many paintings never finished? If the figurine moved or if the intensity of the light wavered, it was impossible to line the shadow up perfectly so as to begin the drawing again.

Why do so many animals look so much alike? Because a single figurine could be used again and again. In any case, many of the animal drawings look similar without being identical.

Why did the irregularities of the walls' surfaces never seem to pose a problem for the artists? Because the shadow was never affected by the surface it was projected upon.

How is it possible that some animals are painted without an outline yet are immediately identifiable? Because the outline is not necessary to create a silhouette; the pigment is sufficient.

Why are some shapes distorted and deformed? These effects are naturally produced when the shadow is projected at an angle onto the wall.

These many answers to our questions still don't explain the meaning of the cave paintings, but they do represent an important step forward in what we know about how they were created. The reader of this book may find when looking at images of parietal art, that he approaches the paintings with a fresh look. No longer enigmatic or even unsettling, the drawings now take on a new coherence and are striking for both their logic and their beauty and their ability to touch us emotionally. With each image now, we can almost see the artist at work and we understand all the mysteries that formerly eluded us: the interruptions, the approximations, and the perfect half-outlines, which an unsteady flame could never bring to fruition. We can imagine the regular unfurling of the outlines, the order in which they were made and the details that were added later, with more or less skill, to fill out the silhouette's contour. Every art has its professionals and its amateurs and so too with the cave paintings; every artist, no matter his talent, will find a kindred soul here.

With so many enigmas resolved, one question takes precedence over all: why did no one ever think of this before? The answer is so obvious now that it seems almost suspicious that it was overlooked for so long. Yet this is exactly what happened: not once was tracing ever proposed as a possible hypothesis, in any of the studies or books written on the paintings, not even in a footnote or an endnote to one of these. None of the researchers or specialists I consulted, no more than their predecessors of a century ago, ever admitted to considering this theory; rather, they all confirmed for me that the thought had never crossed their minds, even though they admitted that any number of technical elements of the drawings had always been problematic for them. Were they too mesmerized by the evocative power of the paintings, too enraptured by their beauty to either imagine they could have been created so simply or to admit that parietal art was a distant relation of Chinese shadow puppets? The idea that these images are nothing more than the mere tracings of shadows could diminish their marvelousness if we failed to acknowledge that the fascination that these magnificent paintings still hold for us today comes from a far more visceral place than a rational one. What visitor to the Sistine Chapel who stands spellbound before this masterpiece of Italian Renaissance art worries himself over Michelangelo's technique?

It should be said that the "how" and the "why" of parietal art has fallen out of fashion in recent years; all the latest studies have focused on painstaking descriptions of the paintings—the hoof of a single horse, an auroch's antler—as if everyone had resigned themselves to the idea that they would never understand the meaning of the paintings or how they were made.

It would be an error to ignore this tracing technique, however, which explains the genesis of nearly all the cave paintings, because it opens the door to fascinating new avenues of research that should lead to further discoveries about Paleolithic art, whose astonishing modernity, it bears repeating, continues to fascinate.

For example, computer imaging and simulation will be able to recreate the caves sufficiently well to clarify several points: how each drawing results from the projection of a shadow on a wall; the characteristics and the position of the flame; the size and the form of the figurine; the precise spot in the cave where it was placed; the angle at which its silhouette was projected; the distance in height and depth between the light, the statuette, and the wall, and the degree to which any of these leaned . . . All these elements may help us see the rooms of the caves and the means employed by the artists from a whole new perspective.[20]

Again, the virtual simulation of the figurines used for the drawings will make it possible to categorize the statuettes that were pressed into service at different times and in different sites and to understand the chronology of their use. Computer imaging would also make it possible to create "hard copies" of all the kinds of animals sculpted and which compose what appear to be the huge frescoes of the caves, but which are, in reality, separate compositions, as proven by radiometric dating.

---

[20] On the other hand, it will be difficult to find evidence of the figurines' position on the fragile ground of the caves. The earth would have been covered over and beaten down by the excavation work completed after the caves were discovered, to facilitate visitors' movement through the caves or to ventilate the space.

Although it will probably never be possible, due to the age of the existing figurines, to connect with any certainty individual paintings to the statuettes used to make them, the figurines and their fragments could also become the subject of new scientific interest: what kinds of shadows can be cast with them and what drawings are they likely to have created? This research could perhaps shed new light on other sculptures like the Paleolithic "Venus" figurines, whose strangely shaped, faceless forms have been discovered all over Europe.

The tracing method can have a practical use as well in the facsimile caves planned at Chauvet (where visitors will be redirected, as at Lascaux, to protect the original site from the kind of microbial contamination caused by humans in the caves).[21] Could there be a better, simpler, and more economical way to create the drawings in Chauvet's future visitor center than by employing the same method used with such ease by the Paleolithic artists? The developers of the planned replica of Chauvet would be well advised to take note.

For all these reasons, I had to share my discovery of the preferred working methods of the Cro-Magnon painters. My idea may challenge some preconceived notions

---

[21] Lascaux was permanently closed to the public in 1963. Altamira was similarly closed in 1977 before being reopened a few years later to allow a very limited number of daily visitors.

and run up against other longstanding theories, even ruffle a few feathers, but it lays to rest the hypothesis of a painting "school" that would have trained generations of itinerant artists who would have been dispatched to various sites across the European continent. The supposed existence of "professionals working for the benefit of all"[22] was recently invoked again to explain the paintings of the Coliboaia cave in Romania and their stylistic similarities with the Chauvet drawings, even though the two caves lie 1,500 kilometers from each other, as the crow flies. The resemblances of the drawings at Lascaux and Altamira have also been explained in this way, by positing exchanges between tribes on either side of the Pyrenees Mountains who would have shared certain conventions of drawing they would have learned thanks to the transmission, among nomadic Paleolithic peoples, of an artistic training spread to apprentice artists by teachers ("professionals [. . .] probably exempted from daily chores"[23]). Very recently still, a specialist asserted rather romantically that schools and training sites existed as far back as prehistory: "This ability to create such lifelike animals, thanks to an assiduous drawing practice, must have seemed purely magical to the people who lived at Chauvet. It is very likely, moreover, that the painters at Chauvet were, as has so often been the

---

[22] Brigitte and Gilles Delluc, *op. cit*, p. 184.

[23] Brigitte and Gilles Delluc, *op. cit*, p. 32.

case in the history of art, thought to be *extra-ordinary* beings, or even living gods (*divino artista*). [. . .] Just as dexterity and observational powers vary from one individual to another, even after a long training period, it is not unthinkable that, as far back as prehistory, some painters could have been renowned for their individual talent and could have enjoyed certain privileges as a result."[24]

Training, an education even, with professors, students, apprenticeships, a school; the only thing missing is an art academy. And now in place of these virtuoso artists expertly trained by master teachers, a perfectly simple explanation would substitute mere workmen practicing an easy to learn, infallible technique . . .

The style and the resemblances of the parietal drawings, even over millennia, should no longer come as a surprise. It is far more plausible that the homogeneity of the paintings results from a procedure that was so easy to learn and to implement that it could be used and passed on over time and vast geographic areas, creating a "style" whose essential features would remain unchanged for many millennia, as well as a method as intuitive as creating the outline of a hand by blowing pigment over it.

---

[24] Emmanuel Guy, *Préhistoire du sentiment artistique. L'invention du style il y a 20 000 ans.* Presses du réel, 2011.

It would be equally wrong to infer any scorn on my part directed at these ancestors of ours who left us the "Sistine Chapel of Prehistory," as Abbé Breuil named Lascaux's Axial Gallery, whose drawings span both sides of its vault. On the contrary, to endow these ordinary men with innate artistic talent they never possessed any more than we do today is to keep them at arm's length by declaring them to be supernatural beings invested with either exceptional powers or an innate science of drawing (which does not exist, for that matter) or gifted with a formidable memory that would have allowed them to retain all the characteristics of an animal's complex morphology and to reproduce them perfectly in their own drawings, even as they assumed the most acrobatic positions in order to draw in the caves. In a word, the theory of an art school refuses to admit the painters were human beings just like us.

On the other hand, we pay them greater respect by recognizing both the ingenuity they showed by using shadows to their advantage and the savoir-faire they demonstrated by developing a technique from their observation of how forms throw shadows when illuminated from behind. As hard as it might be for us who rely on electricity to share their awe, the play of firelight and shadows would have been a source of mystery and wonder for the artists working in the caves. They did not content themselves with mere outlines, moreover; the manner in which they embellished the silhouettes with color and detail shows that they possessed an undeniable aesthetic sense and an appreciation of beauty. To concede they had recourse to a tracing technique rather than freehand drawing does not diminish in any way the value of their artistic production, no more than rote copies minimize the status of the original works that served as their model. At this early stage of Humanity, the technique made it possible to create very admirable works of art. The silhouettes were only the foundation of the drawings; the individual artists colored them in their own way, with their own style, and often with considerable talent, as the variety of the details and the subtle choices of color of the finished works bear witness. Despite the millennia that separate these paintings from us today, these seem so modern, so evocative, that there will always remain one regret: that none of the artists ever left an image of himself or of one of his contemporaries.

A last word on the subject of the artists' skill: even before the paintings, there were the figurines, sculpted with extraordinary finesse, that lent their silhouettes to the drawing process.

XX

Before making my discovery known, it seemed wise to put it past as many people as possible, in the hopes of preempting any later objections. After organizing my notes, I wrote up an argument defending my position in the form of an illustrated dialogue, which I then shared with anyone I knew, of all ages and backgrounds. My fears were unfounded, however: no problems were identified, other than the one that had troubled me, when I too had questioned why an idea this simple had never before been considered.

I sent a few letters to official scientific organizations but no response came. A journalist I contacted who specialized in the subject explained to me that, even if he was personally convinced by my explanation, it would never be accepted unless it were proven by irreproachably scientific means. Then I had a lucky break. Asked to draw the portrait of Antonin Artaud for the cover of *Histoires littéraires*, I found myself in touch with Jean-Jacques Lefrère, a professor of medicine and a literary historian, who was also the editor of a number of periodicals for which I had, in the past, made some illustrations. He was interested in my research and we decided to determine together whether my methodology could stand up to questioning. We began a scientifically rigorous, systematic review of my findings that aimed to uncover the slightest weakness in my reasoning and the least bias in my interpretation of the results.

We began by testing my hypothesis several more times from the phase at which the shadow is projected on the wall. We had at our disposal a veritable zoo of different figurines (a horse, a bear, a bison, a cow, a bull, a rhinoceros, etc.) and we asked a dozen or so friends and family members who had no previous training in graphic art to participate. We gave each of them a piece of charcoal and asked them to trace shadows under all the kinds of conditions we could imagine: drawings with the figurine placed upside-down, intermingled drawings, superimposed drawings in great number, anamorphosis, etc. We asked our participants to add finishing touches (eyes, ears, noses) to the inside zone of the outlines but always using the same light source as when they traced the shadow, and they were challenged as well to refrain from drawing the outline but to apply color to the shadow with the palms of their hands.

The results of this first experiment were completely convincing: working under the same conditions known to the prehistoric painters—as least as we could recreate these, while sparing our guinea pigs the chore of having to crawl through narrow tunnels—all the participants were able to draw the figurines' outlines confidently and to color them in easily. They also experienced no difficulty in creating animal silhouettes without the outline that proved as easily identifiable as the paintings at Lascaux and Chauvet.

Our next task was to compare our participants' drawings with the originals in the caves, at least as well as we could study these in specialized books. Our intention was to reassure ourselves that all the different particularities of shadow tracing could be found in the original drawings, but the results were overwhelmingly positive. Everything matched. There can be no argument to the contrary.

Jean-Jacques Lefrère also took upon himself the task of reviewing all the available literature on the subject of the paintings. Again, not a hint of my hypothesis was found but we did locate a few interesting suggestions of the same idea which, without approaching the question from quite the same perspective, indicated that we were not the only ones to have considered the idea. The most notable hypothesis was developed by a photographer named Matt Gatton, who tried in 2006

Techniques of Cave Painting in the Paleolithic Period

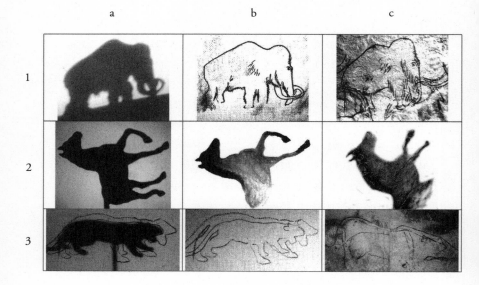

By line, from left to right: shadow of the figurine (a), traced outline of the figurine's shadow (b); comparable prehistoric drawing (c).

1c: mammoth at Rouffignac cave – 2a: shadow cast by an upside-down figurine; 2c: the "Upside-Down Horse" at Lascaux – 3a: shadow projected onto a wall bearing a similar drawing; 3c: superimposed images of lions at Chauvet

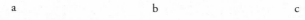

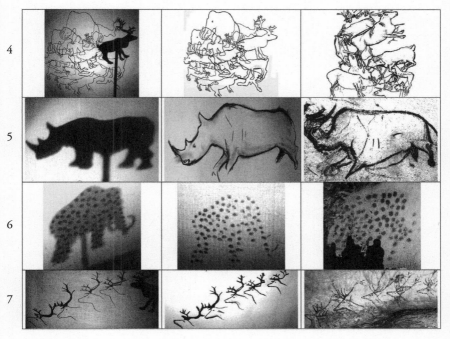

4a: shadow projected onto a wall bearing multiple drawings; 4c: prehistoric drawings in the Room of the Little Reindeer at Les Trois-Frères (from a tracing made by Henri Breuil) – 5a: example of anamorphosis using a rhinoceros figurine projected at an angle; 5c: rhinoceros at Chauvet – 6a: shadow cast by a mammoth figurine, filled with red ochre handprints; 6b: resulting drawing with shadow removed; 6c: wall bearing handprints at Chauvet – 7a: projected shadow and resulting drawings of the same figurine, reproduced five times; 7c: frieze of the "Swimming Deer" at Lascaux.

to apply the famous principle of the *camera obscura*[25] to certain types of Paleolithic art.[26] Behind this idea is the well-known principle of the pinhole camera,[27] which preceded the invention of photography as well as some

---

[25] "By allowing the light from objects to penetrate by a small hole into a darkened chamber, it is possible to capture the images of those objects on a sheet of paper placed there [. . .] although their images will be reproduced smaller and turned upside-down." (*Traité de la peinture*, Berger-Levrault, 1987, p. 168.

[26] Matt Gatton, Leah Carreon, Madison Cawein, Walter Brock, Valery Scott, "The Camera Obscura and the Origin of Art," *Proceedings of the XV World Congress UISPP, Lisbonne, 4-9 September 2006*, vol. 35.

[27] Leonardo da Vinci, who described the camera obscura, explained that the images produced by the pinhole camera are much smaller than the original objects that reflect the light into the box. The principle of the pinhole camera is also at work in heliography, as developed in the nineteenth century by Nicéphore Niépce: the very brief projection of light (exposure) through a hole makes an image on the light-sensitive emulsion coating a sheet of paper (film). The pinhole camera that Gatton imagined Paleolithic man might have known, and which he dubbed a "paleo-camera" is therefore an early ancestor of a kind of "photography" that is made by hand in a very reduced format.

early attempts at cinema: by the means of a small, round hole punched in the side of a closed box or room, whatever that hole can "see" of the box's exterior surroundings will be projected onto the wall opposite the one with the hole, appearing there as an upside-down image. According to Matt Gatton, a similar, accidental projection of an image onto the wall of a tent in Paleolithic times could have inspired the artists to want to preserve those images by carving or drawing over them on a flat stone. It's an interesting theory, one that could explain the many figures with blurry features found in large numbers engraved in stone at certain prehistoric sites.

Unfortunately, the same principle could hardly have been used inside the caves, and certainly would never have been employed to create the very large drawings that are sometimes found there. For the principle of the camera obscura to function, there must be a concentration of powerful light rays, such as during daylight hours. The only way to obtain a similarly strong light source with an oil lamp would be to project the light through an optical lens, such as those used today in film and slide projectors. Without such a lens, the image could not be seen or would be so faint as to make tracing it impossible. In any case, there is no evidence that such lenses were known, used, or could even have been produced, some thirty thousand years ago.

If this technique more closely resembles the magic lantern,[28] what Matt Gatton's theory does point to is the intuition that some form of projection must have been used, and that this idea occurred to at least one researcher. But the kind of projection he proposes is so difficult to pull off and so ill-adapted to a cave that has no natural light source that it does not explain the technique used to create the cave paintings: in the absence of a lens, the image created by a camera obscura is not only far too small but its outline would be so faint and blurred that it would have been the most mediocre of tools for creating a shadow that the artists could have traced.[29]

---

[28] Antoine Furetière described the *laterna magica* as thus in his Dictionary of 1727: "The magic lantern is a small optical machine by which it is possible to visualize in total darkness on a white wall such horrible phantoms and monsters that whoever sees them but does not understand their secret will believe they have been produced there by magical means. The machine is composed of a concave mirror which reflects the light of a candle through the tiny hole of a tube, at the other end of which there is a lens which lies between two slides on which extraordinary and ghastly creatures have been painted and which then appear, much larger, on the opposite wall." (Source: *Le Cinéma des origines à nos jours*, Editions du Cygne, 1932, p. 17.

[29] The camera obscura could well have served, however, to create the small engravings found on free-standing

Pursuing his reasoning, however, Matt Gatton imagines that the tiny outline of an animal's silhouette, appearing like a "snapshot" of the actual beast would have inspired the Paleolithic artists to create a negative cutout of that silhouette on a soft surface (clay or leather). Light from an oil lamp would have been projected through that stencil and the artists would have traced the outline of the silhouette as it appeared on the wall of the cave.

All things considered, even if this other hypothesis closely resembles certain aspects of my own, it seems totally unlikely. Besides the fact that none of the stencils that Matt Gatton imagines have ever been found—unlike the many figurines discovered in the caves—the graphic possibilities presented by the projection of an illuminated shape onto a dark wall and by the tracing of shadows are not at all the same: the latter technique is far simpler to execute and much more instinctual. For

---

surfaces; the lines of these drawings (choppy marks repeated again and again, animals with multiple feet, so drawn to create the impression of movement) contrast markedly with those of the cave paintings, which are fluid and confident and are always limited to the contours of the drawings. If the existence of a "paleo-camera" could be proven, it would demonstrate that Cro-Magnon man was more interested in optical phenomena than previously suspected.

another thing, throwing a strong light onto the walls would have lit up the earlier drawings that covered their surfaces, and these now visible paintings would have certainly disturbed the prehistoric artists at their work. The technique also would have been prohibitive to creating the varied images at different angles of a single animal in the same way that the incidents of anamorphosis would have been much more difficult, even impossible, to create in this way. Other characteristics of the cave paintings, such as the vitality of the animals, which are often depicted in full gallop, would also not have been possible with this technique, which relies on the creation of a stencil from "snapshots" taken of real life. This technique would have forced the artist to wait for an animal such as a mammoth to cross the line of sight of his "lens" and to offer its best side, so to speak, to the camera, in profile. Next, he would have created a cutout of that profile that would be precise enough for its projected shadow to be enlarged without revealing any errors. Clearly, this method requires both luck and a highly skilled artist and presents any number of problems to be determinedly resolved over many millennia. The process described by Matt Gatton—long and fastidious, involving many steps requiring a sure level of skill—is a poor fit with the sheer number of drawings in the caves and the span of time during which the practice was employed. The stencils alone would have necessitated the steady hand of an excellent artist, while the notion of a succession of teachers and pupils engaged in the transmission of a complex technique, over hundreds of generations, seems improbable. The hypothesis is certainly interesting and intersects our own observations but makes the error of approaching the problem in reverse, so that the experiment, which only explains a few of the cave paintings, takes precedence over an explanation for the entirety of the drawings present in the caves.

XX

With the encouragement of Jean-Jacques Lefrère, I undertook a few more experiments, which I filmed, made more and more drawings, and took many photos. Our observations, which we frequently shared, were always in agreement. When we had what seemed to be a sufficient body of proof, Jean-Jacques Lefrère decided it was time to defend what for him had become a certainty: it was through a process of projecting and tracing shadows that the Paleolithic artists had composed their wall art. It was easy enough to convince me of the importance of publishing my discovery, since it explains one of the oldest mysteries in the history of mankind. From his perspective as an academic, however, it was crucial that any discovery should be examined by the scientific community, and so this book was written with him.

XXI

"The reasons which inspired the people of the Upper Paleolithic Period to create these splendors remain unknown, and probably always will be so," wrote Pascal Depaepe in his book *La France du Paléolithique*.

In fact, knowing how the cave paintings were made does not explain why they were created in the first place and many more questions persist: what is the meaning of the paintings and why were they made in the darkest, most remote parts of the caves, for a period of many millennia? Why are animals the unique subject of the drawings, to the exclusion of any human, plant, or mineral, and why is the range of animals depicted so limited? Paleolithic man must have had his reasons to paint this way, over such a vast expanse of time, in such inhabitable locations. Finally, what is the meaning of the abstract symbols found on the same walls?

Historians of the Upper Paleolithic Period have put forward many theories to explain the paintings' symbolic significance, long lost to us, but none of these theories has been more illuminating than the rest. The first explanation ever proposed considered the drawings to be simple works of art. By any modern standards, there is a perceptible level of artistry in these animal paintings, but did aesthetic notions hold any sway for Paleolithic peoples? It is a strange kind of art indeed that is hid from view in the deepest and darkest zones of the caves. In the history of humanity, have there been any other examples of generations of artists working out of sight of their communities?

Abbé Breuil interpreted this secrecy as evidence of magical practices by which prehistoric man attempted to dominate the animals they lived amongst, either by hunting them successfully or by making them more plentiful and accessible. He argued that the spears depicted at times with certain animals were proof of his theory, but never explained why so few of the animals are shown in this way and why none seem to suffer for their supposed injuries. The sole exception is the wounded bison spilling his entrails in the Panel of the Wounded Man, at Lascaux. In any case, the idea that the animals shown in the paintings were the primary food source of the prehistoric societies is contradicted by the unlikeliness that they ate lion and rhinoceros. What's more, if a link exists between the drawings and what these people hunted and ate, the range of game depicted in the drawings is decidedly limited: evidently, neither birds, rabbits, boars, or warthogs ever showed up on their plates. Archeological digs have shown that the Paleolithic societies relied mainly on reindeer for their protein source, but these grand animals are largely absent from the cave paintings. If it was indeed a question of improving their chances on the hunt, many other kinds of animals would be represented while others would not be depicted at all. The animals that provided their food are not the same ones that appear in the drawings. For example, Cro-Magnon man hunted many kinds of birds but none are ever shown in the paintings.

By the same logic, the drawings could not be interpreted as scenes intended to celebrate the exploits of hunters or to protect them, since many of the animals shown are not dangerous to man.

For other specialists, the caves must be the sites of initiation ceremonies preparing young men for the challenges of the hunt. The narrow passageways and the difficulty with which some rooms can only be reached are cited as evidence in support of this theory. In fact, many paintings are located in places that require considerable physical effort to be accessed but that bear few marks of human presence, so that it appears that these areas were visited only infrequently, or at least were not the sites of large occult gatherings. In fact, it would appear that some rooms were only ever visited by the artists themselves. André Leroi-Gourhan was convinced the caves functioned as sanctuaries of a kind, but he had no explanation for the fact that certain galleries were almost certainly only used once. Indeed, the theory that these caves housed magical rituals hardly concords with the evidence: why would the prehistoric artists go to such lengths to leave only a few drawings and then never return there again?

As for Leroi-Gourhan's structuralist theory, which holds that the drawings are organized by species, size, and orientation on the wall, to form panels depicting a whole mythology, it is no longer thought to hold water, just as his binary hypothesis regarding a male-female duality and a bull-horse paring is equally discredited today. But in 1970, on the television program *Un certain regard*, this respected professor at the Collège de France applied lengthy statistical analysis to his ideas about the kinds of animals depicted, their juxtapositions, and their presence in each cave. The complexity of his interpretation seems ill-suited to a practice that was handed down for more than twenty thousand years and cannot explain those panels whose drawings were added over many millennia so that certain paintings on the same wall are much older than others. Yet, for almost half a century, Leroi-Gourhan's structuralism was the leading theory and even became for a time the only explanation for the cave paintings. Today, it has fallen out of fashion entirely.

Shamanism has also been invoked as a possible explanation for parietal art, perhaps because it is among the oldest spiritual practices, but there is no archeological foundation for this theory and there are few proponents of it today. Reptiles and birds are present in nearly all shamanistic rituals known in the world, but these are curiously absent from the wall paintings.

The cosmogonic theory espoused by Chantal Jègues-Wolkiewicz holds that the Lascaux site was chosen for its entrance, which is lit up by the setting sun at the time of the summer solstice, and that it represents the prehistoric solar system.[30] According to this hypothesis, the paintings in the Hall of the Bulls represent the constellations, but this has never been confirmed by any specialist of prehistory, and it isn't clear whether the same argument could be made concerning the other caves.

Could the paintings be the work of extraterrestrials? Even that possibility has been raised. If aliens exist, there's no reason why they might not have been interested in human societies beginning in prehistoric times, and they might have enjoyed a mammoth hunt to boot.

This is a good note on which to end our catalogue of possible theories as to the meaning of parietal art. If there is one thing that all the specialists can agree

---

[30] Chantal Jègues-Wolkiewicz, *Sur les chemins étoilés de Lascaux*, Editions Pierre philosophale, 2011.

on, it is that the animals of the caves undoubtedly were painted for a reason, albeit one which remains to be elucidated. And since there are so many theories out there, most of which were developed over the last few centuries, why not throw a new one into the fray?

And so we do, but with a caveat: unlike the experiments described earlier here, we should be clear that there is no scientific evidence for what we are about to postulate. This is an idea only, complete conjecture, in fact, and perhaps little more than a fantasy, but it does rest on experiences and deductions that are grounded in logic and observation. We leave it to our readers to decide if our theory seems as improbable as the ones discussed above.

Once again, we went back to our big books about the cave paintings. We had already studied these in the hopes of understanding how they were made; perhaps these offered clues to their meaning as well. What did we find there? For the most part, we saw very beautiful images: elegant deer, powerful buffalo, splendid lions, impressive mammoths. Not a single reptile or toad or insect and no ugly or repugnant or unpleasant animals to look at. No "dirty" or coarse animals either (pigs, boars, warthogs . . .), and no rats or mice or even that feared night-stalker, wolves. In fact, none of the animals shown would inspire fear or revulsion. Moreover, they are always captured in noble poses: whether they are galloping or standing still, they always manage to look dignified. Never is an animal painted in the act of defecating, for example, or copulating, or even shown grazing or devouring its prey. All seem to exude remarkable qualities: strength, vitality, elegance, speed, power, beauty—characteristics, in other words, that everyone wishes to possess. It's as if the animals shown are not actually animals at all, as any reader of La Fontaine's *Fables* knows. In fact, the absence of any human beings in an art form practiced over so many millennia could be explained very simply: the animals are symbolic representations of people.

Prehistorians have long posited that the nomadic societies of the Paleolithic Period were composed of clans—a horse clan, a bison clan, a deer clan, etc.—and that the tribes had to split regularly to survive. For example, if food supplies were scarce, large tribes were more vulnerable to famine, so new clans were formed and these would cross paths with each other as they traveled. Perhaps they would fight or maybe they would discover that they were allies or relations. To do so, however, they would have needed a way to recognize each other, a name to call each other, in order to be feared or respected or acknowledged at all. An animal would make a perfect emblem and its characteristics—strength, bravery, courage, speed—would come to be associated with the tribe's members. Who would challenge the Mammoth tribe, feared for its strength? Who would declare themselves braver than the Lions? Imagine a meeting of the Deer and the Bulls; they would know from each other's emblems that they were allies rather than enemies and they could go their way in peace. Every clan would have one or more figurines carved in the shape of their totem animal to identify themselves when necessary. Their insignia would function as a kind of *passe-partout*, or talisman, and would be invested with a symbolic power that would testify to family ties. This hypothesis would certainly explain the presence of the many ivory figurines that have been found in the Paleolithic sites.[31]

What relationship could there possibly be to the caves? We may know little about the manners and customs of our prehistoric ancestors, but we can be sure that any practice that withstood thirty thousand years—almost a thousand generations—had a good reason for being. The prehistoric hunter-gatherers were not sedentary; they had to regularly move their camps to survive, following the migrations of the wild animals who provided their food and the materials for their tools or their clothes, according to the seasons and the

---

[31] A parallel could be drawn with the emblems of the Gauls or the Romans, such as the boar or the eagle of the Senate and People of Rome, which would be borne on flags, standards, pennants, and banners. This ancestral tradition of displaying tribal affiliations by means of symbols could be passed down from generation to generation.

abundance of the surrounding vegetation. Neverthe-less, these generations of nomads (a few dozen per cave) always came to the same sites and decorated these with their drawings and paintings. What that means is that these specific locations were important and were chosen as the right places to practice an immutable tradition that managed to survive unchanged for thirty thousand years. Of course, no tradition would last that long if it were not indispensable. And if it were indispensable for so many millennia, there is reason to believe that it is indispensable to us, too, and that equivalent practices exist in all known civilizations.

What examples are there, then, of cults that have been practiced over thousands of years, regardless of changes in political structures, religious beliefs, or philosophical traditions, in all environments and climates and regions, through any kind of calamity? There is only one, uni-versal to all mankind or nearly so, that has endured and continues today, and this is the practice of burying the dead and remembering the deceased in cemeteries and necropoles. This is the only "tradition" that has survived the test of time with the same consistency.

For ten thousand years, that is to say since the Neo-lithic age, which was when the prehistoric tribes first settled down to practice agriculture and animal hus-bandry, we have buried our dead in locations specifi-cally set aside for that purpose. Prior to that were the Paleolithic peoples, who were hardly backward, and who resembled us so much already, in their morphology and their cognitive abilities, as we know from their tools, hunting strategies, and lifestyle. It's not unreasonable to suppose that their emotions and their fears did not differ fundamentally from ours either, so that the accidental or natural loss of a loved one could not have been any less painful for them. The search for food obliged these itinerant clans to travel long distances, but not to burden themselves with a corpse: the rough conditions of their existence would have forced them to abandon their dead wherever they died. As a result, no "cemeteries" have ever been found dating from the Paleolithic age.

Once the body was laid in the ground (or perhaps incinerated) and the tribe had continued its route, how could they remember those who were no longer with them? How could they mourn? We find it an intolerable idea to bury our loved ones in a strange place without any record of their passage on this earth or any way of remembering them. Imagine leaving behind a cherished elder on a snowy mountain pass after a lengthy ascent that he was too old and frail to survive. After covering the body with stones to protect it from marauding animals and laying it in a wind-ravaged rock shelter, the tribe would need to find a way to preserve his memory. This they would do in special caves devoted to remembering the dead. When warmer weather would lead the tribe back to the region of the cave, and since the elder had belonged to the deer clan, they would paint a majestic deer, large and bold, on the wall, and the departed ancestor would rest in peace because his clan had paid him homage. At the time of their visit to the cave, they might also paint a smaller deer in a corner to remember a five-year old child who had frozen to death the same winter, or leave a hand stencil in memory of a stranger the tribe had found half-devoured by animals near the river, once the snows had begun to melt.

Hasn't the same tradition survived to our day? Many a lost sailor has had his name engraved in a church in Brittany. The deceased who are cremated are frequently remembered with a plaque in their name erected in a place of remembrance. The most obvious example, however, must be the profusion of monuments to fallen soldiers.

The caves are cemeteries where no corpse has ever been laid, where prehistoric man remembered members of his family or his clan in forms ranging from simple sketches to mark the passing of a vagrant to a huge, carefully painted picture for a revered chief. In cemeteries all over the world today, similar distinctions are clearly visible.

Every beast represented on the walls stands for a human being. Anyone lucky enough to visit the caves has reported an inexpressible feeling of reverence, while many have referred to these sites as "sanctuaries." Their powerful emotional response does not come from the paintings so much as from the impression of eternity that any memorial inspires. This may explain why the caves were never the object of vandalism during the entire Paleolithic Period; the notion of defacing a cemetery is universally sanctioned and always has been. We leave our dead in peace or risk offending their spirits.

That is to say that these homages to the dead were perhaps not inspired only by good will or affection for the deceased: prudence may have advised pacifying the spirits of the dead so as to prevent their ghosts from haunting the living. Fears of the dark or of phantoms, primitive terrors that are still deeply rooted in our subconscious and which we struggle always to overcome, certainly bothered prehistoric people as well and may even have been more intense. Depicting the deceased in the form of the clan's totem animal, in the most remote recesses of a cave, could have been a way of containing the spirit of the dead in a safe place. Once this ritual was completed, the living would no longer fear the ghost of the dead person and the torments it could inflict. There could hardly be a better place to carry out this sacred ceremony than in the darkness of a cave where not even a breeze could reach (which was also, we now know, a precondition for creating the drawings). Without light or movement, the caves could already be the realm of the dead. For these prehistoric people who rose when the sun rose and slept when the firelight was extinguished, shadows must have had a troubling significance, interpreted perhaps as the double or the soul of whatever projects it. Whenever a shadow wavered on the cave walls, it must have seemed to imbue life into the innate object that created it. Immobilizing the flickering shadow with a drawing would have certainly been a powerful gesture: the capricious shadow of the sculpted figurine told the artist where on the wall it should remain for eternity. Then, with a steady stroke of his charcoal, the artist traced its contour carefully and reverently on the surface of the wall, where it would take its place among earlier paintings, some already centuries old, dedicated to the memory of so many forgotten dead. Instead of laying flowers on a tomb, they would have added pigment and details to embellish the drawing. As soon as the ritual was completed, the clan went on its way.

If mankind has always paid homage to its dead with a ceremony and a place in which to remember them, for thirty thousand years, men did not dig graves; they painted them. This simple practice would have persisted for millennia, without undergoing any significant changes. Of course, a practice that can withstand three hundred centuries is as essential to human survival as making fire or fashioning a lance or braiding a cord. Are there any perceptible differences between how the Neolithic beekeepers harvested honey and how modern ones do today? Very little, in fact.

The paintings have survived, unlike much else from the period. But of the many civilizations that are now gone, there is one common thread: the necropoles.

Once upon a time, lasting monuments were only built for the dead. Besides the fact that the caves protected these "tombs" from the aggressions of time and human contact, the only thing that has always been respected, feared, and avoided even is the realm of the dead. Why would prehistoric man have been any different? It's true that they sometimes effaced or covered the reminder of a distant ancestor by superimposing the silhouette of a recently deceased "deer" over a "bison" who died in ancient times. We do much the same thing in our cemeteries, replacing older and degraded tombstones with new ones.

If the caves were painted over millennia, they are not painted any longer. Such a venerable tradition expressing a fundamentally human need and passed down for so long does not just go away from one day to the next, or even from one century to the next, without a major event rendering the practice useless or obsolete. Parietal art ended precisely with just such an upheaval: the transition from the Paleolithic Period to the Neolithic Period, which ushered in farming and herding, and ultimately the sedentarization of the societies pursuing these practices. No longer hunter-gatherers, they constructed villages and settled durably in those areas whose resources they controlled. From that moment on, they could bury their dead close by, in specially designated plots, and remember them by erecting stones and tumuli on their tombs. And they could visit these places. The vast majority of "recent" civilizations have buried their dead in cemeteries (necropoles are only a few thousand years old). Sedentarization marked the end of the parietal art, when there was no longer any need to paint the symbolic forms of animals on cave walls to remember the dead. The caves ceased to be visited and harbored their treasures in silence until they were brought to light for an admiring though puzzled new public.

Two observations confirm this interpretation. The first is the omission of any human presence in the paintings.[32] Since it was impossible for the dead to pose in the caves so that their shadows could be projected on the walls, the clan's animal emblem was used instead. The second is the absence of sepulchers in the vast majority of painted caves; only a few exist (at Cussac and at Vilhonneur in the Dordogne and Charente regions of France, respectively) and neither has been dated to coincide with the period of the cave paintings.

I wondered also if there were any texts from Antiquity that made mention of the practice of shadow tracing, if only in a long-lost legend. Do we understand the

---

[32] The caricatural human profiles found in certain sites or on some remains present too many similarities with the stylistic conventions for caricatures in fashion over the last few hundred years to not be considered with prudence.

real meaning of Plato's Allegory of the Cave? He had it from one of the last Pythagorean philosophers who insisted on its ancient origins.

"Our mistake comes from seeing only what lies before us rather than realizing that the light comes from behind us." This might have been the best epigraph for this book, especially since, with the shadows our ancestors drew by torchlight, the "myth of the cave" suddenly takes on new meaning. The shadows thrown by the light of their oil lamps in the caves would have been the first performances experienced by prehistoric people.

In the same way, could we have ever guessed that the lovely story that Pliny the Elder told about the invention of drawing hides an immemorial truth? "It happened in Corinth, and owes its invention to his daughter who was in love with a young man who was leaving to travel abroad; she traced the shadow of his face projected onto the wall by lamplight."[33]

Prehistoric specialists who might be open to the idea that the animal drawings were made to remember the dead could also provide a new theory regarding the innumerable "signs" engraved or painted on the walls of the caves. Once considered to be no more than a kind of prehistoric "graffiti," or rough sketches of everyday objects, or vestiges of magical practices even, these signs

---

[33] *Histoire naturelle*, tome XXXV, 151–152.

are completely incomprehensible to us today because we are at a loss as to how to interpret them, as we once were with Egyptian hieroglyghs before they were deciphered by Jean-François Champollion. It's too much to hope, however, that a kind of Rosetta Stone will be discovered for the cave paintings that would help us read their ideographic "writing."

These signs are composed of a variety of geometric shapes, thirty kinds in all: grids, circles, rectangles, tectiforms (in other words, resembling a roof), aviforms (in the shape of a bird whose wings are spread), etc. Also visible are lines of varied composition: dots, cupules, bars, and aligned dashes, which all seem to be systems for counting. Because of their proximity to the cave paintings, these signs must be somehow related to them and could hold important information about the drawings, or even a date. They are present in conjunction with the whole of Paleolithic art: on the walls but also on furnishings, and especially on the figurines found in the caves, where they might indicate the identity of the owners of the statuettes.

If we could decipher the meaning of this other form of parietal art, perhaps we would better understand the lifestyle and the reasoning of the people of that period. We usually only see in them a kind of "gentle savage": crude, wearing animal hides, communicating through guttural, inarticulate sounds, hunting mammoths, and taking shelter in the caves, whereas all the known evidence uncovered in archeological digs has pro‚ quite the contrary.

Today, there exist some painstaking inventories of these signs, but no promising theories have been established. No one has been able to say for sure if they are a kind of alphabet or whether these supposed ideograms are in fact the oldest known samples of writing, in as much as writing was formalized some six thousand years ago. Our interpretation may not be factually supported but there is no denying the fact that the signs accompany the drawings nearly everywhere. That means that if our hypothesis is more than pure fancy and these engravings have a meaning in conjunction with the drawings,[34] then the whole of what we can see on the walls of the caves could well have a commemorative or votive function for the tribes' deceased, rather than a merely aesthetic one, and they could be a link between the living and the dead[35] that would explain

---

[34] That the signs have a meaning and that it might intersect the meaning of the paintings is generally admitted by the scientific community.

[35] Reflecting on prehistoric burial rites in his book, *La France du Paléolithique*, Pascal Depaepe, Scientific and Technical Director of the Institut national de recherches en archéologie préventive (National Institute for Research in Preventive Archeology), remarked that, "Paleolithic art may well be one such expression" (La Découverte, 2009, p. 141).

why animals are depicted to the exclusion of humans. The engravings could also have been part of a ritual in which visiting tribes left their "signature" in the caves (much like modern visitors to churches will sign a visitors' registry). If there is a Champollion today who could decipher these signs, we would perhaps learn that an engraving below a horse meant this: "The members of the horse clan came to remember their elder. Twelve people were present."

The manner of thinking and of expression that is now known as parietal art was practiced over the entire Upper Paleolithic Period and was a remarkably elaborate means of communication that was far more efficient than oral transmission. The proof is that it has survived to the present.

XXII

Ever since Altamira was discovered in 1879, prehistoric cave art has always been questioned: its authenticity, its age, and even its existence have been challenged. The discoveries that would follow were not always treated with much more respect. More recently, even Chauvet was kept secret until all suspicions of forgery could be dropped, yet its supposed age, as confirmed by radiometric dating, was called into question because this marvelous cave changed everything we knew about parietal art.

Such skepticism was certainly necessary for a scientific foundation to be laid, and time eventually proved the original incredulity false. Nevertheless, the disbelief that at first accompanied the revelation of these unique vestiges of mankind was responsible for irreversible degradations and transformations that have damaged both the paintings—by preventing their reasonable protection—and our knowledge of this mysterious art.

If our book may open new avenues of research, it may be hoped that it will not meet with the same defiance that experts have so frequently shown those who have dared to venture into the field without holding the requisite credentials to do so.

But the paintings are not solely the domain of archeologists and specialists in the latest relevant fields. There is good reason why prehistory fascinates so many: mankind first expressed itself in these drawings. And so, knowing that the human beings of the Upper Paleolithic Period had at their disposal a technique for drawing that was so simple a child could do it, and imagining that they drew and painted to remember their dead, just as we still do today in our way, confirms for us that no matter how many millennia have passed, we are one and the same humanity, with the same strengths and weaknesses, the same talents, and the same limits.

We wish to thank in so many ways, Carole, Clément, and Sylvain David; Jean-Jacques Egron; Pedro Lima; Jean-Pierre Lassalle; Patrick Berche; Muriel Louâpre; Hugues Marchal; the readers of Adrien Nil's blog; and of course the illustrator Boulet. Our gratitude goes out also to the volunteers who participated in our first, never-before-tried experiments, as well as to everyone at Editions Fayard: Olivier Nora, Sophie Hogg-Grandjean, Sophie de Closets, and Jean-François Dauven.

Photo credits

Figure 1: The Hall of the Bulls, Lascaux, copyright Ministère de la Culture et de la Communication, Direction régionale des affaires culturelles de Rhône-Alpes, Service régional de l'archéologie

Figure 2: Anamorphic rhinoceros, Chauvet, copyright Chauvet/Brunel/Hilaire

Figure 3: Cow with Collar, Lascaux, copyright Ministère de la Culture et de la Communication, Direction régionale des affaires culturelles de Rhône-Alpes, Service régional de l'archéologie

Figure 4: Rhinoceros with repeated outlines, Chauvet, copyright Chauvet/Brunel/Hilaire

Figure 5: Lions, Chauvet, copyright Chauvet/Brunel/Hilaire

Figure 6: Bison, Chauvet, copyright Chauvet/Brunel/Hilaire

Figure 7: Lions, Chauvet, copyright Chauvet/Brunel/Hilaire

Figure 8: Frieze of the Deer, Lascaux, copyright Ministère de la Culture et de la Communication, Direction régionale des affaires culturelles de Rhône-Alpes, Service régional de l'archéologie

"The Chauvet cave was discovered on December 18, 1994, by three spelunkers: Eliette Brunel, Jean-Marie Chauvet, and Christian Hillaire."